The
Star Crystal

The Star Crystal saga: Book 1
second edition

DC Daines

This edition is dedicated to my wife and kids, who have allowed me the time to complete my works, without too much complaining.

artwork by Keith Pennell

All the characters, events and situations portrayed in this book are fictional. Any resemblance to actual persons, living or dead, events, or locales is entirely coincidental.

THE STAR CRYSTAL
Copyright © 2012 by DC Daines
All rights reserved.

Original Creative director and Book design by Evonne Hew
Revision of book design, DC Daines

No part of this book may be reproduced in any form or by any electronic or mechanical means including information storage and retrieval systems, without permission in writing from the author. The only exception is by a reviewer, who may quote short excerpts in a review.

Website: www.thestarcrystal.com
Facebook: the star crystal

Toonlancer artwork: http://toonlancer.deviantart.com/

Author portrait by Daryl Olsen
https://www.facebook.com/ASourcePhotography

First edition: January 2012
Second edition: May 2014

Acknowledgements

Thank you to the three women who helped me mould this book into what it is today. Ellie, Sarah and lastly, how could I forget my mother. In her eyes, I finally did something right. Well almost, right mum?

I would also like to take a moment to thank all those that have inspired me to push myself further. Time and again I have questioned my writing, and time and again, I have been raised up by those supporting me. As such, you should take pride, knowing that this revision is dedicated to you.

Without my Guardian Angel, Bron, my new path would not be possible, for this, I thank her from the bottom of my heart.

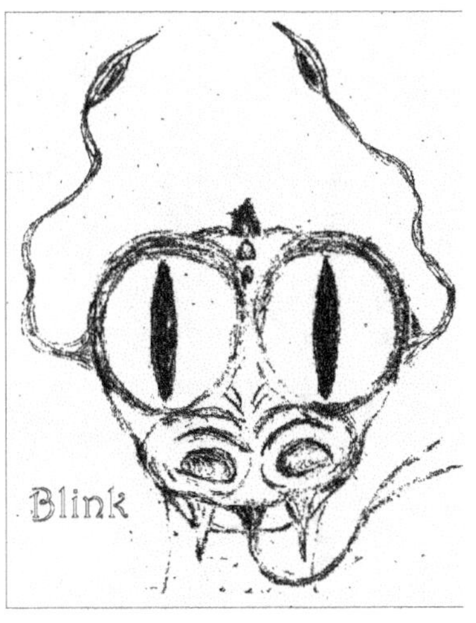

Illustration by DC Daines

About The Author

At thirty four, I decided there was more to life than twelve hour days at work. Three years and a lot of edits later, here I am. Writing is my passion, but the real enjoyment comes from family and friends after they read one of my scenes. Whether it be their faces lighting up, their laughter, tears, or just them calling me names, many of which I cannot put to print. Let me tell you, more than one of them has inspired my imagination and characters in my stories. With two kids, a boy and a girl; I am looking forward to the good times, the hours of jumping on the trampoline, watching their gymnastics, and being inspired by their little stories and colourful depictions of life.

Illustration by Toonlancer

Now if I don't mention the wife, she may think I have forgotten about her, well hardly. Without her there to tell me to get off the laptop or the gaming console and go to sleep, work, or even eat; I may have become a skeleton, sitting in front of the screen.

Prologue

"Before. Before there was dust. Before the air became poison. Before the Company! Our people lived and lived in peace. " The deep throated growl rumbled from under the hood as the cloaked figure's head swept from side to side, addressing all who huddled around the fire.

"Our land… full of life, beautiful life, a life like no other that came before or will come again." The figure paused a moment to amplify its voice, harsher, louder it continued; "That life was taken, taken by force, subterfuge, taken from us; from those we love…we loved." Crouching lower it stared into each of the faces of the crowd in turn. "Now we are lost, a dying breed lost to the decades, the centuries, most of our people barren like our land." Long majestic arms gestured openly to the crowd. "You, our young, some of the few, the only future, the only hope."

Flames from the fire reflected off the black eyes in the same red glow. The vertical slits of colour in each set made them seem young…innocent, but somehow old beyond their years as the voice lowered again. "We must be careful, diligent, blend in, but never let them in our lives again."

Slowly standing upright from a crouched position, its voice became one with the fire as its words washed over the children. "Those we thought our friends took from us, took the beauty, leaving only poison."

Gesturing upwards, the voice hardened "AND FOR WHAT? An extra credit? Another star base? More power?"

The voice lowered once more and the small children drew closer still as they strained to hear, their fine fur becoming more apparent in the light of the fire.

"Poison! They poisoned our land, then they left! They left sickness. Sickness that did not discriminate between men, women and children. There was little left, nothing but a dying race, a dead planet." The voice became sombre, almost sad.

"Is there anything left for us, we nomads? I do not know, nor do I care. I am but a man, a teller! A teller of the past, not a prophet of the future. The beauty, the pain, all are known to me, all shall be known to you." Briefly, the eyes reflected the fire from under the dark hood. To those that observed, the eyes were dark as the night, lonely, broken and unfeeling. The speech, although seeming passionate, was an emotionless ceremony practised to perfection. Yet the children were frozen, hanging on every word.

"I do not take part, nor do I care to. I am but an instrument, an instrument to link you to your past. I…we; we have lost so much, so listen, open your mind." The long sleeves concealing its hands exaggeratedly closed over its chest as it gestured the children closer still. The flames of the fire wavered as if in response to the moving mass of bodies. "Come closer and I will show you… the beauty, the truth, the loss, so you may know too well the pain of trusting those our race once did."

Slim long fingers emerged from out of the black sleeves. Long nail. No! Claw-like extensions reflective in the fire's glow. They slipped into the coat, effortlessly drawing out a box. At first the box seemed simple, but the trained eye could see that it was immaculately engraved with pictures of dragons and warriors of a forgotten time. It appeared impenetrable, with no latches or locks visible in its blackness as it absorbed the light from the fire rather than reflecting it. The hands held the box as though they had always held the box. The eyes, those black lifeless eyes started to glow, a little at first then brighter and brighter as the box hovered over the open palms. The eyes became more intense than the fire itself. The children restlessly waited, not daring to look away. *CLICK, CLICK, CLICK,* the box opened. It fell to the floor, *CLUNK,* but no one heard, nobody saw. In its place floated a crystal shining a million different colours. Wavering images appeared to all who watched. Pictures so beautiful the children were mesmerised. Saplings sprouted from the light to dance upon it. Their crystalline structures settled as they grew larger, sinking deep in the ground, branching out as they filled the landscape. The plains filled with crystal grass and insects so unique they made the children's eyes light up in wonder. Amongst it all appeared the most beautiful beings they had ever seen. With pointed ears and little tails, the children projected to all were naked bar the natural fine fur covering their bodies, glistening in the dim light. Their facial features feline in appearance. They were playing, playing while longer, sleeker forms of them were lying under the sparkling trees, smiling with the brightest light coming from their eyes.

The children around the fire were dirty, tired and worn, their clothes in tatters. These were the children of their children and those before them, yet the resemblance was hard to see. Hard to comprehend how such beauty could end up here, so ugly, on the hull of a lifeless station, floating in the cold darkness of space. As the images intensified, the children's eyes continued to fill with light, showing a distant resemblance to the race before them. As the image zoomed in it became obvious that this crystal, wondrous as it was, was but a small piece, possibly a shard of one of the original trees.

"Strays," The voice booming from the night was loud, military-like, emotionless, the figure invisible in the dark. "Get 'em, now." It was a command not a request.

The crystal's light dimmed enough for the children to be released from its grasp. They suddenly resembled the race they had just seen, their pointed ears pricking up in alarm before bounding away from the fire with all the grace, power and beauty of their kin, but to no avail. Nets came out of the darkness, netting shot with great force, slamming into the fleeing children and forcing them to the ground. Pinning them where they were moments earlier bathing in the light. The attack was planned, controlled and precise. From the pandemonium that had started, there was now only order. All who had tried to flee were now trapped. The teller, the only one standing, the only one not tangled in these evil nets.

The teller's claws twitched as he tried to disengage himself from his trance; the crystal light dim but still controlling him. He could see the carnage, the children lying helpless, he himself powerless to act, his throat lumpy. Movement; one had not been captured. Horror filled his eyes as he could see all that would happen again. The little one started shaking, with hot tears pouring from its eyes. The teller's own eyes swelled in response. Suddenly the child sprang out into the dark only to be slammed into the floor by another of the heavy nets, the assailants still not visible. The teller's eyes became enraged, hatred and anger filling them. The crystal's light intensified again, the images dark and evil, those of a barren wasteland, of corpses on the ground, mass graves, dust clouds and swirling winds. Red dust seemed to be everywhere, blanketing the light. No life, only death, then snow storms, blizzards forming a blanket of white. This could not be the same place, or could it?

The teller's body arched forward violently, hissing a spine chilling warning at the unknown assailants. His hands grasped the crystal, touching it for barely a second before images flashed before them of pain, of death, of tragically wrong choices… Of ships in battle, fighting, snow, blizzards, ships falling…falling. Finally red. Explosive red! Like the light from a sun. His body glowed like the crystal, levitating in the air. The cracking of his joints could be heard over the fire's crackling as his upper body was wretched backwards, his hood and arms thrown back with the arching action. The face revealed was feline, majestic, masculine and proud. The eyes opened. Intense beams of light shone from them, burning the souls of all those who would dare look. Without warning, his body was thrown violently backwards, slamming into the metal bulkhead. *CLUNK!* His mind pained, his thoughts broken as he lay confused, blood oozing out of his pointed ears. Blackness slowly crept in as he watched. Watched as the children, his children were carried away. As the last one was carried off, he opened his hand. The crystal, laying there grew dim, until finally the light went out, as did his.

The smouldering fire barely lit the lean figure as he bent over the box. Picking it up he fondled it while quietly observing the area around the fire. The signs of struggle were all too short-lived, the pool of blood behind him the only sign of casualty.

"Any day now I will have you, any day now."

The voice was full of boyish joy, of a man on his first hunt. Thrilled yet controlled. Standing up, the man moved off quietly, slowly, letting the box slip through his fingers and into the fire as he departed. The flames, striking back up, tried to engulf it. The box was not worried by the fire, not concerned, not changing. The man exited as quietly as he had entered, straightening his uniform as he left, no one the wiser as to his visit, no one to see the flames spark up one last time to light the insignia on his vest.

The Company's brand with its eye's glistening menacingly in the fire's last breath.

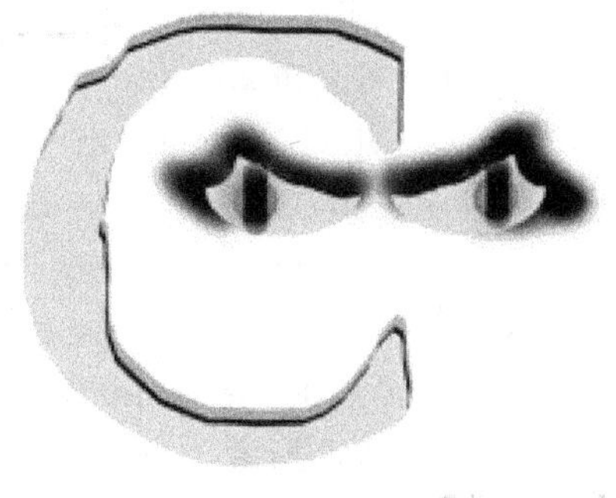

Chapter 1

The air was cold and crisp, giving the large man's breath the appearance of thick mist as it poured from his open mouth. His chest heaved in unison with the billowing clouds in an attempt to provide the all important oxygen to his struggling lungs. Seemingly alive, the clouds were engulfing his features as if attempting to consume the multitude of thin, crystalline icicles attached to his five o'clock shadow. As he stroked this ginger stubble, he stood there, leaning on his rifle, resting his weary body.

His eyes, red from the cold, opened slowly, his pupils set in brilliant blue eyes, quickly dilating as he peered into the distance, trying to focus as he thought, *where is it? It has to be here.* Knowing the odds of survival were poor, he had still travelled to this planet in search of his goal. He knew that he and little else could survive for very long in this barren and cold place, but he had to find something, at all costs. Feeling he was no closer to this goal he had stopped to recuperate after days of searching. It may not have been wise though, to rest here in the deep snow. It swallowed him, covering his calves, causing his legs to go cold and numb. His tall stature, already reduced by the snow, seemed further dwarfed by the large hills that towered all around him. He stood there amongst the silent giants like a ghost in the night, there in spirit but not in body, the snow and coldness numbing all of him. Even his mind!

Fumbling with his rifle, he fell forward, the numbness of his hands hindering him as he…

…tried grasping it. Tears streamed down his face, blurring his vision. His innocent, blue feline eyes sparkled, the limited light through the slats in the wardrobe doors giving him little help to see to grasp the rifle. He fumbled again as it dropped further, his jacket sleeves unrolling to cover his tiny hands and

making it impossible to pick it up. Clunk, *the rifle hit the floor as the doors opened.*

"Shhhh little one. Don't shriek."

"He's always been a little shrieker, hasn't he?" The large man placed his hand on the boy's head, messing his hair as he spoke. "Hush my little boy, they are coming."

Bang! Bang! *The sound of fists on the door echoed through the room, then stopped, only to be replaced by hideous screaming.*

He reached out his hands, the jacket dropping down and over them as he flung his arms around his mother's neck. He lost himself in the soft fur on her face, nuzzled into it, never wanting to let go as she wiped his tears delicately away. She grabbed at his shoulders, gently pushing him from her and locked her eyes to his. "You must protect this with your life, little one. You must." She stroked the butt of the rifle. "And remember the stories. They are our lineage, our burden, our destiny and now yours." Her voice, like an angel to the boy, quietened with powerful effect as she spoke the last words.

Bang! Bang! *The aggressive screaming of the men had stopped outside only to be replaced by a deafening crash as they rammed something against the door in an attempt to break it from its hinges. The tall, thin man swooped down to floor level, desperation on his face and compassion in his voice as the door creaked under the pressure of the barrage. "Come my love, we must leave him. They must not find him, or all we have fought for is lost. They are only after us. Goodbye my little shrieker. I will love you always." A tear rolled down his face as he stood upright, turning to the door as it swung open under the barrage of blows. "Who are you? How dare you-"* Thump, *his father's eyes glazed as they looked across at him, then hollow as he lay there, blood oozing from his skull.*

The look in his mother's blue eyes tore his heart from his chest as she looked deep into his and then adjusted the jacket to conceal him as he cowered. "I am sorry," she whispered as she grabbed the shotgun that lay above the boy's head. She raised herself and turned in one fluid motion as she cocked the chamber and offloaded two rounds into two of the men who had entered the room. Their bodies were flung against the wall amidst a splatter of blood. The little boy lay still, not sobbing any-more, just looking, his eyes hidden by the large jacket as he watched his mother's legs rise from the ground. The man lifting her spoke as she gasped.

"Feisty one, are you not? Half breed, I will have to teach you a lesson and it will be my pleasure." Sickness filled the man's voice as he spoke and turned to leave, still holding her by the throat as her legs continued to kick. "Clean up this mess. We have never been here!"

"Yes Captain Garath. And if we find anything of interest?"

"Do what you wish, but be warned. Do not take too long, Lord Dragoon will not be pleased if we are found out."

His body felt numb and his stomach hurt as the boy crawled from the closet. The foul smell of drying blood filled his nostrils and his eyes blurred as he looked upon the red stain on the carpet. Th-thump, th-thump, th-thump. His heart beat slowed as he raised himself from the ground only to fall again.

Screech, screech. The dragging of the rifle echoed down the metal street as the boy made his way along it, the sound resonating as though the voice of a tortured soul. His head was lowered, his shoulders drooped and his body hidden in the large jacket. The strap from the rifle exited the long sleeves giving him the appearance of a ghost, aimlessly wandering whilst dragging a rifle and sporting the empty shell of a jacket.

He was a terrifying sight — no one dared go near. They just shuddered, hurrying away as they heard the shrieking beneath the hood. Observers could place no emotion to this sound as they could not see the tears or the red eyes that sported them. Therefore, they hid their children and scurried away; leaving this lost and lonely soul to walk, to find his own destiny.

"Hey you, give me that!" The voice was high-pitched, the words spat out by the older boy as he grabbed aggressively at the rifle, trying to remove it from this mysterious figure. Not straying from his destiny, the young boy did not respond, did not let go, he just continued walking. The boy screamed his commands again, his larger stature doing nothing to aid him as he was dragged behind. With the rifle still in his hand, he tried pulling it from the moving jacket. "Get me a knife, boys." he yelled to his companions as he continued to be pulled along. Grasping the knife with one hand and the rifle with the other he swung, the blade deflecting off the strap, not even grazing it. "What the?" The boy raised the knife again, this time attempting to plunge it hard and fast into the jacket.

"Whoa there, Tristan. You want a hiding?" A strange accent slipped off his tongue as the tall gangly man grabbed the boy's wrist as it came down; the knife slicing the jacket. Twisting his wrist, the knife fell. "Be off with you boy, and take your gang with you."

Tristan turned and ran, with venom in his voice he yelled, "Don't turn your back old man, don't turn your back," the group of boys following.

Kneeling down, the man removed the hood and his heart skipped a beat as he saw the small boy's face before him, the sight heart-wrenching. Bloody tears stained the child's expressionless face, the white of his eyes blood red. "I am Philippe, who are you?" The boy lifted a hand, placing it on Philippe's face, smearing blood as he did.

"Phypee." The boy lowered his hand and Philippe gasped at the bloody sight.

He ripped the jacket from the boy to check further for wounds. Finding none, he asked. "Is this your blood, boy?" Philippe waited as the boy looked blankly at him.

"Phypee." The boy pointed again, still looking distant.

"What is your name, boy?" Philippe spoke softly as he lowered himself to his knees.

"Phypee." The boy pointed to Philippe again and then to himself. "Scrycher…"

"Scrycher." the voice whispered in his ear. Absently he grabbed at his eyes trying to pull himself out of his slumber. "Scrycher, we have been called to the chambers." He swung around and sat up, only to lean forward sleepily. His eyes barely opened as he rubbed them and scratched at his ginger bum fluff on his chin. Philippe patted him on the head as he mumbled. Not able to raise himself, he could not see Philippe, looking down affectionately. This sleepiness was lost as he heard the scraping steel of the large knife removed from its sheath. Wide eyed he caught the glint of its razor sharp blade as it was slipped into his belt. "Better not keep them waiting."

"Philippe, you have been accused by another agent of the Syndicate. How do you plead to the charges?" The young man spoke strongly as the fire burnt high within the room.

"Not guilty." Philippe turned, pleading to the man as he ran his slim fingers through his greying hair. "Gregory you know me, I would not do such a thing."

"Then there is only one way to settle this. A duel to the death." The last words were barely audible over the roar of the crowd, now rising in anticipation of the coming event.

The voice whispering in his ear was as cold and unfeeling as the thin blade that now poked into Scrycher's back as he stood watching the trial.. "I told him to watch his back. When he can no longer protect you, you had better watch yours."

"Philippe I will take your place, it is a set up. I believe I know who is behind it." Scrycher pleaded with Philippe as his large muscles flexed in agitation.

"No, Scrycher. You are but a teenager and too hot-headed for your own good. You need to watch the duel and if I am killed, run. Run and do not turn back." Philippe turned from Scrycher, covering the tear in his eye as he reached for the knife in his boot. Thump.

Scrycher was dwarfed by the large man throwing insults as they circled the fire and the two squared off. "You fool; you are no match for me."

"More of a match than Philippe, you coward! Tristan, I cannot believe that even you would stoop as low as this." Scrycher sized up his opponent as he stalked quickly around the fire, making sure each foot was level before he placed the next.

"You should never underestimate the resolve of your opponent Scrycher, especially when it involves climbing the ranks."

"Why does it concern us?" Scrycher jabbed his knife forward, barely missing Tristan's arm.

"You don't know, do you? You are favoured as the next leader. The head of the Syndicate. That is my destiny, not yours." Tristan spat the words, but they were still barely audible over the crackling flames from the fire that concealed them from all but Scrycher.

"I do not want your destiny. I have my own." Scrycher fell to the ground as Tristan lunged, both men rolling together as their knives clashed.

Tristan plunged the knife as he whispered. "Well, follow it."

As he leant against the stones from the fire Scrycher pulled back his burning arm. He rolled as he threw the body from him. Both men regained their footing quickly to continue the banter and fight...

... *"Who are you to tell us where we should live?" the Stray teenager hissed at Scrycher as they squared off again, re-circling the fire; his eyes reflecting the fiery glow as his stance lowered, ready to pounce.*

"Well, umm." Scrycher's voice sounded nervous as he stood off against this Stray gang leader. "I know you have been victimised and you have fended for yourselves in the past, but things are changing, and for the worse."

"Yes, they are changing. I can see this. You are here now, aren't you? In my face and disturbing my brethren." The Stray gestured towards the other Strays huddled around the fire as they waited on his every word. "And you are not even a pure-blood." He emphasised the disgust in his voice by spitting into the fire, its flames rearing high in response. "Who are you to tell us what we have to fear? You should fear us!"

"It is talk like that that has seen our kind hunted through the centuries. I wish you could see my point. We need to make a stand, but not until we are strong enough and not like this. Our people are fractured and we are being

picked off, one small group at a time. There is nothing we can do to stop it yet, but in time…" Scrycher could see that he was gaining the interest of the others so he continued, emphasising the next few sentences. "This is to be our first response and line of defence. This will be our legacy to our children."

"And why should we trust you? Be rounded up like some sort of livestock, to give them a chance to wipe us all out with one fell swoop? We have as much right to live in freedom as you, 'tainted blood'."

"They will not attack such a large group for fear of the repercussions. Their current attacks are being conducted in secret. We need to, OUT THEM, these Goon Squads." Scrycher paused for a second too long as the Stray rebutted again.

"We know of Lord Dragoon's secret militia. We are not afraid. Let them bring their little men and see if they can tame us… We, the untameable, the strong, the chosen. They are but jealous fools."

Scrycher's voice was low as he completed another circle of the fire, now in a low crouch and ready for combat. "If they are jealous, what does that make you?"

"Their nightmare!" The Stray threw his hands up in the air at his last words and turned to the crowd gathered around the fire, who in turn cheered and copied the action.

"You will not join us?" Scrycher's voice was still low as he accepted the defeat, his first assignment not having the outcome he had desired.

"I will not join you, 'tainted blood'." Venom dripped from his tongue as he spat in the fire again.

"What do you fear by joining us?" Scrycher's eyes lit up as he latched onto an idea.

"I fear nothing." The Stray's eyes flared with hatred as he spoke directly into the fire between them.

"Then you will not fear this? Anyone who wishes to join us, please come with me now. You will be protected."

A small Stray boy, a half-breed, better known as a Scrag, stepped towards Scrycher but was stopped by a commanding gesture. "No!"

"What do you fear? You have free will as do these children around me." Scrycher waved his hands in the same motion he had seen the Stray perform earlier.

"We are not children." The voice was strong, arrogant and volatile as he yelled, pushing the small Scrag back into the crowd. "We stay here. We fend for ourselves, we protect ourselves. We are Strays. Now leave!" Finishing, the Stray jumped the fire, landing before Scrycher and grabbing his throat. As Scrycher's head tilted back the Stray's voice quietened. "Before I taste your 'tainted blood'."

Click. *"Enough… Scrycher, we have wasted enough time here. They can find out the hard way."*

Scrycher brooded as he walked down the street. He disliked defeat and even more so, failing at such an important task.

"Cheer up Scrycher, we'll find a way. We always do." A young and attractive, well-dressed woman spoke, a large smile covering her face.

"Always the optimist, hey, Chelsea?" The older, greying man spoke with a slight accent, as he looked around, the area before them suddenly quiet. "I don't like this at all Scrycher. We need to get out of here."

"Always the worrier, aren't you Philippe?" Scrycher put his arm around the two as they stopped suddenly. Before them, a band of black clothed men marched towards a definite destination, ignoring the three completely in their haste.

"No, Scrycher. Whatever you are thinking… No!" Philippe's look scorned Scrycher for what he was about to do next.

"Chelsea, up for a little reconnaissance?" Scrycher smiled ear to ear as Chelsea nodded and they headed off after the men.

"We are the untameable, the strong, the chosen. You do not scare us. We are your night-" The Stray's head rolled into the fire before he could finish his sentence. A young, handsome man lowered his arms and laughed as it did.

"Does anyone else wish to tell me they are the chosen?" The Strays huddled together not wanting to move as the rifles from the men surrounding them were cocked.

"Is that the last of them?"

"Yes, Captain Zackory." The man, mid-thirties, lowered his head as he spoke.

"Well, get this area cleaned up then, man. No witnesses, no evidence. Then meet us back at the ship."

"Yes, sir."

He had waited till Zackory was out of ear shot before he kicked a few items into the fire and mumbled about the injustice of it all. "A glorified rubbish collector, I am." Kicking a large crate, he jumped into the air, holding his foot in agonising pain. With his face red and his shoe off, he attempted to move the crate again, this time with his hands, but to no avail.

Zackory and his Goon Squad disappeared into the distance as he walked around the crate in confusion. Realising there was no back, he placed his hand in; fumbling for a second before he pulled it back, screaming. While flicking one hand in the air in pain he managed against all odds to grab the small Scrag by his mass of hair as he attempted to bolt. "You little … I'd better teach you a lesson." Picking up the struggling boy by his hair, he threw him over the crate, pulling a knife to hold against his throat. "You had better be still boy or we'll have us a problem."

The Scrag lay bent over the crate as the man pulled down the boy's pants. Looking around quickly the man dropped his own before proceeding.

"Better get out of here, Scrycher." Philippe grasped his shoulder as he stepped away, not caring to watch.

"Chelsea?"

"Boss this is too much; let's get back to the ship."

"Ok, I'll be there in a minute." Scrycher stared at the man before him and the action he was going to perform, then something snapped inside his head.

"Scrycher." Philippe turned as he heard the shots. Tooh, tooh.

"Get out of here now!" Scrycher yelled as he jumped over the crates they were using as cover, running at full speed towards the slumped over Goon Squad operative.

Scrycher pulled the man off the small boy who just stared back blankly as he looked at him. "We need to get out of here boy, and now."

"What is your name?" Chelsea stood behind Scrycher, looking into the boy's brown eyes. He did not respond, instead he looked blindly at her. "Call you Scrags then. Until we find a name for you, that is."

Throwing the boy over his shoulder, Scrycher scorned her as he started running. "I told you to get."

"Then who would have kept you safe?" replied Philippe…

"Philippe, I do not know what I can do for them after this. This man Zackory does not give up. He has already locked down this whole station in his attempt to find them. I am surprised you have evaded them for this long." the middle-aged man with jet-black hair and sporting high-quality clothing spoke quietly, his eyes shifting from side to side. "If you were to work for me though, I could maybe send Zackory off the scent, possibly with two bodies to quench his thirst."

"Nefal!" Philippe's eyes showed his disappointment "You know I have to protect him, he is my charge." Philippe looked over to Scrycher who was ruffling the boy's hair and giving him a piggyback.

"I think it is time to pass on the torch, old friend. And you know how I have been trying to get you to work for me, ever since you left the Syndicate." Nefal mumbled about the injustices of having to wait for so long as he turned.

"Done. You had better make sure he is safe, or I'll-"

"Good as done."

"Well I'd never thought of this escape plan, you are good. Should be calling you Nifty Nefal from now on." Scrycher gave the man a hug, ruffling his clothes.

"Don't touch the clothes, don't touch, and don't touch." Nefal jumped back, mumbling again before he spoke strongly. "Now don't worry, it is bigger than it looks." Scrycher closed his eyes as he lowered himself into the cold storage container. The lid closing on him and Scrags as he heard the faint voice of an angel.

"See ya on the other side, Boss. Hope you don't catch a cold." Chelsea's laughter trailed off as the lid was closed.

Scrycher's hands pulsed; becoming clammy, his throat dry as he gulped and his mind soured, panicking at the closeness of the cold coffin. With his senses in turmoil, he searched for something, anything, to latch onto. He rummaged through his pockets for something familiar, anything to touch, to hold. He brought forth an item, but it was not familiar. Lifting his hand from his pocket...

... he remembered where he was, forgetting the ordeals he once faced... The motion of his head ceased as he glanced down at his left hand. Slowly and gently he opened his painfully numb fingers to expose a brilliant crystal. In elegant beauty the crystal pulsated, a myriad of colours illuminating from it as though it was singing a song of life and love; of a long lost lover to be found once more.

The crystal's elegant illumination appeared to be in stark contrast to the large barren hand that held it. The hand was cracked, oily and scarred and gave the observer the feeling that Scrycher was extremely protective of its contents; as though a father of his only son. Ever so gently, as though answering his father's call, the crystal moved its soft ray of light, expanding outwards into the distance. The landscape possessed an eerie glow that the crystal's light cut through like a beacon in the night, penetrating deep into the icy mist.

The light of the crystal seemed much brighter on this dimly lit planet; a planet that should have been in darkness with no active sun. An unnatural radiance appeared to exude from the snow itself, a glow as unique as the planet it covered. This planet was alone as though exiled from all others; with Scrycher, a lone man; wandering on its surface, searching for its answers. Walking with short forceful steps he continued, his feet barely lifting as he pushed them forward through the snow rather than over it, gradually making his way towards the unknown destination with his purpose and intent clear… Find it, find it at all cost!

Chapter 2

The cold darkness of space outlined the ship as though framing it in the sky. Two wings, a cockpit, and storage area in the tail section, traits of a true smuggler class vessel. However, its resemblance was more of a ghost ship than a smuggler's vessel; the captain long gone and no crew visible. Seemingly with no crew to pilot it, its momentum was obtained only from its orbit around the planet, so slow that it looked as if it were skulking. It was a lost soul, screaming from the grave. Its parts creaking and moaning as if the strain on the hull was too much for it to bear. The outer hull appeared battered and scarred, barely air tight, as though a dead shell no longer used. Its scarred appearance resembling that of an old retired veteran vessel mourned at a dock in a ship's graveyard - a veteran who had fought her share of battles, with war stories to tell, but tales never told of victory. Sections of the hull appeared severely damaged. Make-shift plates of sub-grade steel had been welded in place, keeping sections intact and the barely breathable atmosphere inside.

The tiny portholes evenly spread through the crew's quarters of the ship were the only visible sign that life once walked the vessel's decks. From one of these holes, a cloaked figure peered out, looking into the vast deepness of space. *Nothing around!* He sighed in relief; *the Company is not here yet! So there is still time for us to get to our goal before we are found again.* This figure, the storyteller from the fire, turned slightly to face an enormous white mass that their ship was orbiting. The ship was positioned far enough to prevent it from being sucked into the gravity field and crushing its hull, tearing the last glimmer of life from it. The sheer size of it loomed over the vessel, making the ship seem tiny and insignificant in the planet's presence, the ship a mere speck in the dark sky. How barren this planet seemed, nothing of importance to keep Teller's attention. Instead, his thoughts turned to their Captain who, after months of searching, was now on this hostile planet, cold, alone and determined to find their mutual goal! The last few months were a blur for Teller as he had gone from never being in battle to being battle worn; memories flooded back, of trying conflicts and lost friends. Not much else seemed to matter now.

Teller was not the man that had started this trip. His journey started at the fire, his tales told to the young. Then he awoke in the brig, a prisoner; confused and lost. His only purpose before this fateful day was to tell the past of his people; the gruesome past they had all endured, told to those of his kind that had survived centuries of victimisation. He had not wanted any part in this quest to find the homeland, to try and allow his people to be reborn again. But here he was, one of only three remaining, one of the three left alive!

"Don't worry, Teller. He'll be right, always is." An elegant and soft female voice echoed from across the room, the voice getting louder but staying soft as she walked to his side. This woman, although soft of speech, was not so gentle on the eyes. Her face a multitude of scars and the tank top, although hugging her supple breasts did more to show her ample tattoos and wounds than cover them. Many of the wounds fresh and weeping.

The two figures stood staring out the window, both hoping for the best. They knew that the last few months had been nothing but disastrous, their lives going from as normal as they could be in this age, to being ruined; running for their lives, chased by a Company vessel.

"We have all been through worse you know. After all, we are smugglers, and you don't often get a smooth ride in our trade." She cracked a slight smile as she put her arm around Teller affectionately, squeezing his arm slightly, his soft fur parting as the pressure from her grasp wrinkled his robe into it. She liked the silky soft feeling of his fur and the warmth of it through the material. She breathed in subtly, her breasts lifting as she took in the slightly musty odour that was emanating from his fur.

"Chelsea, you know you are more than smugglers, you are like family." A glint of affection appeared in the dark eyes under the hood.

"What you mean? 'Family'?" Chelsea's voice rose to a high screeching pitch.

"I mean-" He was cut short.

"Don't get your fur in a knot. I know that comment means a lot coming from you, Stray." The smile widened on Chelsea's face as the affection became more evident in her expression. This expression lasted only seconds before becoming a grimace as pain from a recent scar afflicted her face. "What happens if we don't find it?" she queried, the pain dulling her optimism slightly.

"All this will be for nothing. Nothing at all! The pain, the suffering will be for nothing." Teller's voice had changed, the past few months wearing it down. His voice was no longer passionate, instead it was tired and worn, but it still held the edge of a storyteller.

"Pity we are so short-handed then or you'd be down there with Scrycher, this whole thing resting on your shoulders as well." The smirk returned to Chelsea's face as she affectionately patted Teller on the back, and turned to leave the room, "Better get back to the cockpit, this thing don't run that great any more, let alone run itself."

Teller watched her glide away, his eyes working her up and down, assessing her supple figure as he purred softly. *If only things had been different* he thought, inhaling slightly. His feline senses were attracted to her lingering perfume, the fragrance reminiscent of some native flower of a forgotten time. His purring stopped abruptly, he knew they were not in a different time and he sensed that things were about to get a whole lot worse...

"Yes Sir, they seem to have been orbiting above this planet for some time, days even. This is very unusual, not like them at all. Because of this, I am being very cautious... I want to make sure that I apprehend them this time." The voice was calm but strained, the words being forced out instead of being spoken with the eloquence common to it. This was the voice from the fire. The single confident lone figure, the Company man, his voice had changed considerably - less excitement harbouring in its tone and far more dread.

"Captain, are you sure they are above the planet?

"Yes"

"One you have not charted before?" The voice originating from the monitor seemed marginally older, though very similar to the first. It was controlled with an underlying need, as if wanting something that was almost in his grasp.

"Yes, this planet is definitely not on the Company's charts, and it has not been claimed. I will know more when we can get close enough to scan it-"

"Blow the ship out of the sky this time then." The voice decisively cut the Captain off, making his desire very evident.

"But, you did not want them all killed, you made that very clear! Otherwise this may have been over months ago. We would not have had to been so careful." The Captain knew that his comment was far from the truth. However this was all he could think of to get this man, this Lord, the one displayed on the monitor before him, to reconsider this rash decision of killing all on board the small vessel.

This Captain did not want any more blood on his hands. The blood already staining them had been from the attempted capture of these criminals. Several conflicts had resulted in combat casualties. He did not feel they were his fault, but it was on his conscience none the less.

"We both know you are a bleeding heart, and that you would not have done things any differently. I just gave you a reason to follow your heart. No longer will I protect you by doing this. You must grow up and become a man. Kill them all, Lance!" The Lord's expression was concealed by the black hood, the harsh tone in his voice the only way of telling that he was not going to take no for an answer. "We cannot have any witnesses to your incompetence, as the Captain of your vessel you must know that! The Company has come too far to have its decisiveness questioned, and allow room for others to revolt against us." This voice kept its clarity but was now raised for effect. "Or do you want me to send one of your brothers to finish the job?"

"What if there are survivors?" Lance, the Captain, was now clutching for a way out of having to kill. This ploy was his only hope. *If we could somehow wound the ship, we could take prisoners.*

"Did you not hear me the first time? It is time to kill them all!" The voice from the monitor was losing its control, slipping a little to allow a disapproving tone to come into it.

"No, my Lord! I cannot do this."

"DO NOT disobey me Captain! Lance, you know what happens to those that disappoint me. You should have caught these criminal scum months ago, it is your fault! If you'd caught them then, you would not have to kill them now. You cannot let emotions cloud your judgement, you are a Company Captain. You are one of the youngest in the fleet, but you need to earn what has been given to you." The voice had become almost ceremonial, like a preacher, preaching to a child.

"Yes. I know you pulled a few strings, I get it. Don't let you down!" Lance's voice had dropped to a defeated tone.

Lance knew this fight had gone on too long, the older voice from the monitor was right, but not for the reasons he thought. They were cunning, smart and loyal to death, these criminals. Only a few remained. Out of all that had been at the start of this chase, maybe three of them still ran from them, the Company. Or were these criminals running to something? They had stopped often during this chase but he did not know what they were stopping for, or what they were running to. He did not know and it did not matter! Lance had been sent on this mission to apprehend this band of smugglers and crooks, arms dealers and thieves. All that mattered to him was to uphold the law by apprehending the criminals and getting them tried and convicted, their crimes punishable by death. He did not want to be the one carrying out the sentence. He was a man of honour and truth, not a murderer. He much preferred to let the courts decide their guilt and fate once he apprehended them. How he wished he were in those courts now and performing his trained profession.

"Well get to it now, Captain Dragoon!" The voice from the monitor was direct.

As Captain Dragoon turned to walk away, the voice finished the conversation decisively. The Lord of all the Company did not like being disrespected. "If you do not destroy the ship, and kill everyone aboard… Do not bother coming back! I will disown you, SON!" It was a strong emotional attack, but he knew it would work. No matter how strong this inexperienced Captain's morals were, it all came down to wanting approval from one man. His Father.

The monitor blinked off before Lance had completely turned around, his appearance reflected on its screen. He was very young, neatly dressed in the Company uniform with not a thing out of place, his face clean shaven and the blonde hair on his head cropped. *Almost over*, he thought and not a moment too soon. He desperately wanted his old life back.

Lance composed himself by removing the creases from his jacket, the creases that in reality did not exist. Then he briskly made his way to the bridge.

"Garath, the spy I have on board Lance's vessel will make sure he does not step out of line, and if he does he will be terminated." Lord Dragoon's voice was calmer now, and his posture was relaxed as he sat behind his carved desk.

"What about the Councill? I heard they are restless." The room behind Garath was dark, with the monitor the only thing lighting his face as he spoke while stroking his beard.

"Just let me worry about them. They only care about living the high life that I help to support, at least for the time being. Anyway, they are so preoccupied with the appointment of Lance to Captain under those unfortunate circumstances that they are oblivious to our real agenda." Lord Dragoon's agenda was clear to him, after all, he was a 'true dictator', his own plans and covering them up was all that really mattered. The

Company Councill would not have taken kindly to the type of activities he was performing, all coordinated and executed in an attempt to raise himself to God status; *well I have lived five hundred years, so why shouldn't I be a God? The time is nearly here to end the Councill, once and for all!*

He was drawn back from these thoughts by Garath's relaxed comment in the monitor before him. "We should have found this planet and taken over the Councill years ago."

Lord Dragoon did not like being questioned and his voice betrayed it yet again as it rose to answer. "Patience! I have been searching for this planet for hundreds of years, another few days will not matter. You forget, we were almost exposed, so as far as the Councill goes, I cannot kill their suspicions yet."

Raising a mirror from the table in front of him, Garath preened his eyebrows whilst speaking in a matter of fact tone. "Zackory can eliminate that problem for you. You know how he likes that sort of assignment-"

"No! Assassination is not an option yet. It is too soon."

Garath's voice rose slightly as he put down the mirror and looked deep into the monitor. "But he is getting bored, and harder to control."

Lord Dragoon dropped his voice slightly, trying to calm the situation. "I need you, as the older one, to make sure Zackory does not return to any such duties, yet. He is somewhat too dramatic for this delicate time."

"Well he gets the job done, doesn't he? Who else could hunt and capture Strays the way he does?"

"We cannot supply the Councill with any evidence of our activities. This is why I have you." Lord Dragoon's voice contained praise as he ended the sentence.

"In five hundred years they have not exposed you, why should they now?" Garath's voice had become teacher like, asking in a very calm and composed tone.

"Power is changing Garath and they can feel it. We will soon be in power and they will be thrown the scraps. This is a good reason to be cautious in itself."

"But Zackory has increased his normal activities again. Since Scrycher's unfortunate redirection planned by yourself, he has been more successful in the raids."

"This is fine as long as he is discreet. As I have said before, we need to quash the resistance's hope by retaking their home world for ourselves. In doing this, the Strays we have not relocated should fall back into the shadows."

"So we can continue to mop them up in a planned fashion, as you have been doing slowly, ever since you came to power. Heard it one hundred times before." Garath slouched back in his chair, his tone bored as he stroked his beard again.

"Oh but Garath, you do not understand. Once we have their home world and have overthrown the Councill, we will have the power to completely wipe out their pitiful existence once and for all. After all, they are no better than animals."

"The time is here to end the Councill, Once and for all! We have almost crushed all hope that has been stirring in the Strays. I have seen to that personally… Brother." Zackory's voice was strong and anxious; he wanted to start killing again.

"Yes, Zackory. With that annoying ship being chased by Lance, our pickings have been more plentiful. But we still do not know where they have hidden the Strays they have removed from under our noses."

"I still say we should kill Scrycher, his crew, and Lance and take what we want from the Councill and our father."

"In time Zackory, in time."

Zackory turned from the monitor with fire in his eyes as he yelled at Garath. "You and your bloody time. Our time is now!" As he turned back in hatred, a black monitor greeted him.

Chapter 3

"What is going on?" The ship lurched sideways catching Teller unawares, stumbling forward he barely correct his balance as he grasped for the unlit control panel.

"They've found us again, the mongrels! Out for blood they are. Already taken two hits, any more and we plummet. Can you man the gun?" Chelsea blurted out as she struggled with the flight stick, not taking a breath as she tried to out-manoeuvre the much larger Company vessel. Even though their ship was fast, she was having little success. The ship itself was old and badly damaged from the months of fighting. In an act of sabotage, Jaxter the mechanic had been killed. The Gatling gun was their only weapon and it had had its effectiveness reduced in the sabotage. The explosion was planned and precise; the saboteur; a slimy Rodent who knew what he was doing. Once a friend, now filth swept into a gutter. With Jaxter gone it allowed for only dodgy or minor repairs to be performed. What little this ship had left would not give them a clear victory against the much larger and superior gunned Company vessel. Their only hope was to take out their opponent's weapons, and run for cover. Cover they knew they did not have!

Teller climbed into the circular cage that was protruding from the ship, a crystal window surrounding it separating him from the dead of space. "Alright, I'm in. Need to get me somewhere near them before it'll do any good though."

"You just be a pesky little mosquito, and I'll worry about the driving. Geez it's worse than being married!" Chelsea pulled the flight stick hard to the right and the ship groaned and shuddered under the manoeuvre.

"If they do not kill us, you will woman"

"Shut up and shoot, you fool."

Captain Lance Dragoon paced back and forth impatiently with the rhythmical clunk of his polished boots echoing on the metal hull of the Company vessel. The sound paused for a second. Stopping to view the ship in front of them, he nervously rubbed his sweating palms together and licked his dry lips as a bead of sweat dropped from his brow. The tension in the air was so thick that the crew could almost hear the sweat as it hit the deck. Lance knew he could not fail again! "Have we taken out their weapons yet?"

"No sir, we have made two hits. No vital components though, whoever is flying that thing is as crazy as hell and we can't get a weapon lock yet." The Gunnery Sergeant was also sweating as he babbled. This ship should have been easy to wound but it was moving too erratically, this situation seeming all too familiar. These criminals had escaped too many times. Even though they were always out-gunned and out-manned, they had always found a way to escape. *With my help of course!*

The order to wound was one that he did not like to receive, but this time, Captain Dragoon gave no other. The Gunnery's other 'Secret Orders' that he had received from the cloaked figure were just as lame. He had not questioned the cloaked man in the past and was not about to now, as the promised reward was great. He remembered these orders vividly.

"Do not kill the Criminals, ensure they get to where they are going. Wound them but don't capture them until I tell you otherwise and there will be a nice payment at the end of it. And whatever happens, do not let anyone know what you are doing." The hooded figure was adamant about that.

Lance had made it easy to follow both men's orders, but at the end of the day there was no place on a Company vessel for a man with morals. The Gunnery knew why Lance had been put in command of this vessel - because of Lord Dragoon... Lance's father! *What gives a man the right to put his son on a vessel meant for killing, when the son will not kill?* He then corrected himself in thought, *men had disappeared over less.* After all, Lord

Dragoon was the head man, the one the Company used to control everything.

While deep in thought, the Gunnery did not see the smaller ship change course, nor did he realise the ship was now heading straight for them. Small, fast moving projectiles hit the dome in front of the bridge, *Ping, Ping, Ping,* shaking the ship slightly. Surface cracks webbed outwards from where the bullets had hit the dome, the external pressure from their cruising speed lengthening them and forcing them deeper. This would have meant a breach on the smaller ship, but not this vessel. The automatic repair system acted quickly, fixing the cracks in the dome to stop it from compromising.

"What are they doing? They know at this range they do not stand a chance. Are they trying to ram us? What are you doing?" Lance could just see it, another failure and another notch to add to his failed record. In his anxiety, he recalled the most recent conversation with his father and yelled. "Stop them. Shoot them down. Shoot to kill!"

The Gunnery Sergeant smiled, forgetting in the moment the 'secret orders' that had filled his thoughts only moments earlier 'to not kill the criminals'. *At last*, he thought. Finally, he did not have to wound the oncoming ship. He was not sure what had changed his Captain's mind but he wasn't about to question the decision. This was why, as he grabbed the firing control harder, his fingers turned white with the pressure. He knew he would make the hit and the hull of the little ship would soon be breached.

"Oh ya wanna play hard ball? I'll play hard ball. Try an' hit me now," heckled Chelsea, as she pulled the ship into another hard turn to barely avoid the weapon fire from the oncoming vessel. The strain of the fight was weighing heavily on her and the ship. Her arm muscles pulsed under the strain, and the hull creaked and moaned intensely as the ship twisted and turned under her control.

"You are going to have to get closer than this if you want me to wound them," yelled Teller from his gun station. "I am barely grazing them." Sweat was already pouring from his brow as the Gatling gun overheated, raising the temperature in his little compartment. The faulty cooling unit installed in the gun was now nearing its critical temperature.

"How 'bout this? Send you straight down the whore's throat." Chelsea pulled back the stick and aimed her ship towards the bridge of the Company vessel, pulling the flight stick this way and that in order to dodge the oncoming assault of weapons fire.

"You're crazy woman, just crazy enough. Keep it coming... straighten up."

Chelsea took advantage of a lull in firing, gambling away her manoeuvrability as she accelerated the ship. Her trajectory was now directly into the glass dome of the vessel before them. *Maybe it will increase our odds, now we get close enough for the bullets to make a difference.* Biting down on her lip, she could taste the blood, as the strain of the manoeuvrings became even more evident, and she tried to block her aching muscles from her mind. "Now!"

Teller pulled the trigger of the Gatling gun which responded by roaring as the bullets sprayed from its hot, angry shaft. They flew like a determined swarm of red insects as they attacked, crashing into the glass dome. Teller did not have time to appreciate this small victory as he spun the gun in response to the counter attack. The firing rod glowed more intensely as he pulled the trigger yet again; sending another spray of bullets toward his attackers. He had changed his aim perfectly and his bullets hit their target, exploding the cannon fire mere metres from their source. The outcome was pure brilliance with the force of the explosion wrenching the cannon from its mooring. A large amount of the hull itself was torn from the Company vessel, it stumbled, pulling down and away from the smaller ship. With their movement diminished, the only option left to her crew was to limp away like a wounded animal.

"Oh yeah, who's the man?" Chelsea was chanting over and over again.

Teller dared to take his hands off the gun as he wiped the sweat from his brow. His hood was soaked through as he butted in; his voice loud and strong in order to be heard over her chant. "I am. You've got breasts and awfully good ones at that, if I do say so... Not that I've been looking of course." A glint of affection sneaked into his black eyes as he looked towards her.

They relaxed slightly, laughing loudly as Chelsea steered their ship back towards the planet and away from the wounded vessel. Exhausted, Teller allowed his hands to rest on the top of the gun. With its column still burning red hot he tried to catch his breath, his eyes watering at the smell of the burning gunpowder and metal.

The steering grew more erratic as the little vessel creaked louder and louder. "Those last few tricks really screwed with her, she won't be doin' that again. We need to get her down there." Chelsea gestured to the planet. "We won't last another attack."

"We won't last long down there either, if we don't find what we are looking for." Teller called out behind him after leaving the gun station. He headed in the direction of the escape pod - the only option left to them if they were to survive.

Scrycher stopped again, leaning on the butt of his rifle in order to rest his weary muscles. The continuous inhalation of the cold air had made his chest and nose feel as though they were burning, and his sense of smell was all but gone. *If only I had a better idea of where I was going, I could have landed the pod closer.* He looked back through the hills and valleys, trying to see the pod. It was but a dot in the distance. *Has it been days?* He did not know.

The snow fell lightly on his face as he gingerly looked up into the dark sky, the cold of these flakes unfelt. He knew his ship was waiting in the dead of space. Waiting for him to come back, to venture home; the ship the only thing he had called home for years. As he was reminiscing, the sky lit up as though a procession of blended fireworks. The colours formed a blanket of light that attempted to enclose the planet. The upper atmosphere and the white snow covering the landscape now acted together, amplifying the light above into a brilliant display. *This is not good!* The display of lights went on for some time, seemingly hours with every light blast sending his heart racing until it stopped abruptly.

His heart slowed, hope was still there. *Maybe they had fought the Company vessel off.* A large explosion lighting the heavens interrupted these thoughts. Two eyes peered out of his pocket in response to the explosion, only to quickly return; too afraid to venture out. The light from the crystal in his left hand became brighter, feeding off the explosion above. His hope faded, but a glimmer, however small, remained as he thought of the possibly that they had escaped in the last pod. Gnawing at the back of his mind was the flawed design of these old smuggler's ships. *It is a long way from the bridge to the escape pods*, but a little hope was better than nothing.

Tearing himself from his thoughts, he shook his head. He had to think the worst! That the Company would be here soon. His only recourse was to find what he was looking for before they found him.

"Not far now." he mumbled to himself through his blue and cracked lips. "I hope."

What Scrycher was searching for was not clear to him, but he did know the story. Folklore, told by the Strays, telling of rebirth and of a second coming for their species. His mother, a part Stray, a Scrag, had told him these stories. They had been handed down from one generation to the next, and his mother's telling of these stories had put him to sleep every night. *Until the night the Company came!* He vowed from that day that he would find the truth of what was happening, and someday find a way to make the Company pay for their crimes against Strays and their families.

On the harsh and unforgiving streets he had learned a trade, becoming a smuggler and moving things for the Syndicate. These were not men you wanted to let down, and Scrycher learnt this the hard way. As dangerous as this profession was, it was the only way to get what he wanted…

information! Some of this information collected had brought him here. Some of it had got them hunted like dogs. The later made it very apparent that there was one corrupt and powerful man behind it all, and that it was he who controlled the Company. This man had been trying to wipe out all the Strays by employing a private goon force to do his bidding. His power reached further into space than even that of the Councill itself. Scrycher had accumulated enough information and was now waiting for a platform to use it. But as the Company's Councill was small and well protected, there had been no way to transfer it to them without putting him or others at risk. He thought he would have had the time to wait for an opening to do this. Maybe he was wrong.

In his complex life, he had helped many others, mostly young Strays. Those Strays that had survived the generations were few and widely spread across the clusters of ships, stations and small polluted planets. His goal, after his time with the Syndicate, was to relocate the young Strays from these places before the Company's Goons got there. It was a difficult task and his ship was not fast enough to be everywhere at once. This was why there were several other ships; ships that helped this cause with none knowing the others identity. With enough ships to evade the Company and to keep them guessing at what was really happening, each of the Strays were collected and deposited in safe havens. Several safe havens existed amongst the planets and stations. These allowed them to store the children like cargo until they could somehow, find somewhere to call home. He had not been able to get to this task lately, to help the Stray people. The last haul of Strays seemed another lifetime ago.

Smiling, he reminisced. That last haul was where he had met Teller. Well, captured would be a better word. *Stubborn little stray* he thought, both of them on a similar goal. One focusing on the past, the other using the past to shape the future and both were carrying the burden of knowledge. Teller was different from most Strays he had met, as he seemed peculiar and older. Maybe it was the knowledge of the Stray people. Of their ancestry and their planet that he somehow knew and carried within the crystal, showing it to all that wished to experience it.

Scrycher had seen one of these displays at the fire where he had first seen Teller. Teller had been projecting images of his home planet, and the Stray people. Images that were stored in this crystal that related to their life, free from pain and suffering. Well up to the point where the Company had crushed them. Generations had passed since the Strays' had a place to call home. There were rumours that the planet had been bombarded with barbaric nuclear devices; rendering it uninhabitable. However, there were no written records of this occurrence, only stories and rumours. All traces of their home-world were now gone, seemingly removed from all written records. The Councill's power was indeed great, as now no one knew of the planet's location, or if it ever really existed.

Scrycher knew the planet must exist, as Teller carried the memories of it in the crystal. The crystal had been the last piece of the puzzle, and with Teller's blessing, they were now using it like a compass to find their home.

How the Captain longed for Teller to be down here with him. This was not to be so, as fate had dealt them a cruel hand. During this chase, the cards they received were poor to say the least. The toll on the crew was devastating for some, and deadly for others. The relentless chasing by the Company vessel had never let up over the long distances they had travelled. Nevertheless, the Company vessel's crew, or Captain, was not ruthless; unlike the Syndicate operatives that had also joined in on the victimisation of them. Many a time Scrycher's ship had been wounded long enough for the Company to take a kill shot, but they had not. Scrycher's crew had waited on these occasions for the final deadly shot, but it had not come. This allowed his crew to be slightly optimistic; to never give up hope and find a way to overcome; to out manoeuvre, out-think and out-run the bigger, more powerful vessel.

They had spent the best part of three months fleeing from this Company vessel. All the time they were running, they were searching for their end goal. Following leads and referencing the stories and information had led them here. Led them to what would be a final showdown, of that there was no doubt in his mind. Which side would win, he did not know, but he hoped that fate had dealt them enough pain and would allow them this one final victory. But alas, this Company crew were different. A normal

Company Vessel would have given up the chase by now as they would have accepted a bribe, or demanded one. However, not this Captain. Captain Dragoon had only wanted surrender from them. Obviously, his father Lord Dragoon demanded no less.

It was because of these constant and un-relentless attacks that many of Scrycher's ship's components were broken. The communications were knocked out and the hull had to be continually repaired. Many a makeshift plate was now welded to the hull after close encounters. The hull was now looking like one big breach. As if the shoddily welded plating was not bad enough, the weapons and pods were all but destroyed. One pod had been destroyed in battle, the other claimed by a meteor storm they had been forced to enter, to escape a Syndicate vessel. The same storm that took the life of little Scrags…

"Scrags. Scrags. Don't move." Scrycher raised his rifle quickly as he yelled, pointing it at Scrags' messy head of hair. *"Profitor. What do you make of it?"*

"W-well Scrycher. I-t seems t-to be s-some sort of lizard." Profitor's voice shook as his eyes beamed and he grasped at his beard, stroking it very quickly.

"Not like any bloody lizard I've seen. Shoot it boss." Chelsea stood close to Scrags, leaning back slightly as the small creature hissed and screeched at her from its perch in his hair.

"Enough!" Scrags yelled as he grabbed the small creature by his snout and looked deep into its large bulging eyes. *"Enough, naughty, naughty."* With a small flick of his finger, Scrags tapped him sternly on the snout and let it go.

The creature shook his body with his tail whipping around before he lowered himself as if to sleep.

"N-no Ch-Chelsea." Profitor was too late as the creature turned on her approaching hand and bit her before it disappeared.

"Shitten little rodent. When I get my hands on it I'll…"

"D-did you s-see that?" Profitor stuttered, pointing at the little creature that was now back on Scrags head again; this time with a small silver cloth that it dropped into Chelsea's hand before it returned to its attempted sleep.

"What you reckon it wants?" Chelsea used the cloth to bind the small bite as she spoke.

"Blink wants to sleep. He'll be right when he warms to you." Scrags continued on his way through the clearing and towards the ruins.

"Have you seen him before?" Scrycher looked curiously at the boy as he spoke.

"No."

"Then how'd you know what he wants?"

"He told me so…"

"Sc-Scrycher, you need to see th-this." Profitor had made his way through the little glade and into the temple like ruins. He now stood looking towards the centre of the room where a metal cage on a pillar was surrounded by a pool of mud.

"What do you reckon belongs in there Prof?" Scrycher stepped closer, studying the pillar while pointing to the metal cage.

"A-A power s-s-source ma-maybe."

Scrycher pondered as he recollected the tales from his mother. The cage, the power, the map, the crystal, "What about **the crystal**?"

"P-possibly. W-we w-w-will need i-it-t t-to find ou-out."

"I reckon I know just the man to help us find it."

"The crystal and the Story Teller are here, Scrycher. You will need to be quick if you are to meet up with him. He never stays in one place for long." The voice over the console was quiet but anxious, his accent thick.

"Thanks Philippe, I owe you one." Scrycher signalled Chelsea as he turned from the console confirming their new destination.

"Just one, Scrycher? You know better than that."

"We'll catch up with you, and settle it over a drink once we get that crystal."

"I'll hold you to that, son."

"Off to get the crystal, hey boss?"

"The Crystal and our destiny, Chels." Scrycher's voice trailed off as he repeated, *"Our destiny."*

"Boss, what we gonna' do with 'im?" Chelsea nodded towards Teller. *"Can't leave 'im here or he'll get Gooned for sure."*

As Scrycher walked over to the unconscious Teller, he replied. *"Leave him to me. I'm sure I'll find a use for him."* Picking him up by the arm, Scrycher effortlessly threw the body over his shoulder, the weight barely registering as his muscles rippled in the firelight. Teller's limp body flopped around allowing the crystal to fall from his grasp and clink on the metal deck below.

Blink's attention was diverted from his attempted nap as the crystal clinked on the deck. His eyes enlarged so they looked as though they were all that were on his head. His head raised, his ears rotated back and forth, looking and listening for the source of the pretty sound. He did not see the crystal until Scrags had it in his hand, its light getting brighter as it was placed into Scrags' pocket. Blink's neck curved over Scrags little head and down towards the pocket inquiring.

"No Blink, not yours."

As Teller raised his pounding head, he looked deep into Scrycher's eyes. *"I will help you. But if I find out that you are working for the Company, or your own selfish gains, then I will see to your demise. This is our ancestors' planet we are searching for, not another place to profit from. Understood, smuggler?"*

Scrycher stood up and extended his undamaged hand as he laughed. *"I'll hold you to that."*

"Scrycher's laughter was stopped by an explosion so loud it caused ringing in his ears. He turned looking at the cockpit area of the ship and the smoke billowing from the door.

"On it, Captain." Jaxter jumped, sliding over the large table as he ran for the kitchen to grab a large extinguisher and continued his forward momentum into the cockpit. Swwwssssshhhh. The sound of the extinguisher filled the room as the smoke changed colour and started to thin out. Jaxter's face was becoming clear in the smoke as he spoke. "See Boss, told you I'd-" The smile across Jaxter's face was the last thing Scrycher saw of him as another explosion erupted through the cockpit. The sound of the explosive force was only diminished by Jaxter screaming as his leg flew over the table and slammed into the wall behind Scrycher. The screaming silenced, and the rest of his body splattered over the ship's walls, and the others in the galley.

Scrycher dropped his rifle as he desperately tried to wipe away the blood from his hands, as if trying to remove a stain. Failing to do this, Scrycher turned, red faced, raising his rifle again in an intensely threatening fashion. As he screamed, spit sprayed the dead body of the Syndicate man he was standing above. "First you sabotage our Gatling gun, which kills Jaxter. Then you tell me that you traded his life for this gun? You filthy rodent. You need to be swept into the gutter where you belong." Scrycher looked deeply into the eyes of the man standing beside him, searching for something; regret, some link to a soul. Seeing none of these, he raised the blade from his rifle, swinging it downwards to land one decisive blow.

"You are dead Scrycher. The Syndicate will hunt you." Turning quickly and dodging the downward thrust the man ran, disappearing into the darkness of the streets.

Teller turned, ready to make chase, but was stopped by the impact of Scrycher's furious voice. "No Teller. He will get his own. Let us get out of here now, or our mission will end here."

"Almost there. Lucky everyone else is aboard." Scrycher looked back as the gates closed and they neared the ship, stopping suddenly as something caught his eye and he cursed.

"Well, well, what do we have here?" Gregory easily grabbed the smaller Profitor by the scruff of the neck. "If we cannot have the master, we will have the slave. SCRYCHER!" Gregory's voice boomed Scrycher's name over the sound of the rain. Teller now turned to watch, gasping at the scene through the bars of the gates. "When I catch you, I will do this and worse to all your crew."

Gregory threw Profitor into the man beside him.

"B-but I-I th-thought w-w-we we-were f-f-f-friends."

The man pulled his knife from its sheath, glaring at Scrycher as he pulled the knife across Profitor's throat.

"I have no friends!"

Scrycher cursed continually as he stormed through the ship. "I thought I told him to get back to the ship. I made that bloody clear, did I not? The bloody imbecile." Scrycher was fuming as he reached the cockpit. The comment was rhetorical, so he did not waste time waiting for an answer, he just turned and stormed off to his quarters. "Get us out of here and in a hurry."

"What 'bout Rod and Profitor Boss?" Chelsea questioned quietly.

"They're dead Chels... they... are dead!"

"Get to the escape pods and make sure they are ready to launch. They may be our only way out of this mess." Without questioning Scrycher, Scrags ran through the cockpit door and into the galley towards his destination.

"This is Gregory, and I want your surrender. Oh, and do not try to run or we will blow you out of the sky."

Scrycher nodded at Chelsea, signalling his reply. She answered by throwing the ship forward, violently accelerating and causing the rest of the crew, except Teller, to fall to the floor. The large battle cruiser returned the prior verbal statement by opening fire on the tiny ship trying to escape its clutches.

"Into the storm Chelsea, it is our only hope."

Chelsea did not hear Scrycher, nor did the rest of the crew as a meteor smashed into their hull, amplifying the ringing in their ears...

The small ship limped its way out of the meteor storm. Many of its plates had been torn from its hull; but the bulk of the little ship was, for the most part, intact.

"Scrags, you can stand down the shuttle pods now." Scrycher turned around searching the cockpit area. "Scrags? Scrags, where are you?"

"Scrycher, one of the escape pods is missing. And I think Scrags was in it."

"Aaargh, Scrags. What have I done?" Scrycher murmured as he remembered their blight...

All these incidents meant the ship was nearly defenceless and the crew downtrodden. This had definitely been a hard three months. The crew had been diminished to three tired individuals just wanting the chase to be over.

Scrycher's only hope of victory was to locate what they were searching for. In order to do this he needed to leave his two crew mates on the ship. The crew then reduced to two. Two would be needed if there were a fight. Two would be needed to make a last stand. Two standing between him and them… He needed to hurry, to find this thing they were searching for before the Company found them once again.

"Yes, Sir. The hull has almost finished repairing itself. The compartment it ruptured has also been repaired so we have got power back to navigation."

"What about the cannon?" Captain Dragoon's voice hardened, aggravation creeping into his voice as he thought aloud. "How did they evade us again? They must have nine lives." The slight amount of guilt he had felt when giving the order to kill had washed away when he had to face his crew again. Another defeat! The embarrassment was clearly written on his flushed face. Another evasion from this band of criminals was completely unacceptable.

Lance was dreading the looming call from his father, Lord Dragoon. He had not heard from him yet. Long gaps between communications were not uncommon though. The Company owned all of the space colonies and surrounding planets and his father was a busy man. Lance was not sure why Lord Dragoon was taking so much interest in this particular chase. He had originally hoped that it was interest in his own son's life, his life. Unfortunately, it seemed that this was all about something else as it always had been, ever since Lance was a child. He was pulled back from these thoughts by the answer to his question.

"No, Sir! None of the cannon was left on the hull. As you know, we require part of the object to be left intact to be able to replicate it back into place. The resulting explosion of that last shot removed half the hull." The Gunnery Sergeant's voice betrayed his nervousness as the sweat beaded down his brow. Allowing the ship to get that close and get a shot off was an obvious mistake on his part. Knowing how to handle the situation was academy stuff. Not even a cadet would have been so foolish as to let another ship get that close. He had done many things like this in the past, and Captain Dragoon seemed not to notice. Lucky for him, Lance's natural incompetence was making his sabotage of their mission much easier.

"Can we start moving again, Gunnery Sergeant?"

" We can, shortly, Sir." The Gunnery's voice became evasive as if hiding something. "I'll just need to double check a few systems before we head off." This was not the whole truth, but a distraction from his real agenda. The Gunnery waited.

"Dismissed!" Lance's voice was still agitated. He knew that the longer they waited, the more chance there was that his father would call and the subsequent lecture would follow. "Let me know when you are ready to finish the hunt." He headed towards his quarters, striding off in his normal pompous fashion.

The Gunnery Sergeant stood restlessly fondling his jacket buttons in the dark room. On the opposite side of the table stood a dark, menacing figure, his features obscured by the black cloak and hood adorning him.

"You have done well to help sabotage the capture up to this point but your orders are now rescinded. No more chasing. You need to kill them now. Do you understand? All must die, whatever the cost. We now have what we want. Once you perform this last action, your payment will be deposited in your account, waiting for your return home." The very young but mature voice sounded much like Lord Dragoon's. He did not pause to allow the Gunnery to answer. The Dark figure only required one thing; obedience!

The Gunnery did not care that the figure did not want him to speak, or even who it was, giving him the orders. He did not even think to speculate about who it could have been under the hood. All he cared about was leaving this life, and collecting the promised final payment. "Yes, Sir" The Gunnery left the room promptly, smiling ear to ear. His mind filled with ways he could spend the riches he was to receive, thoughts going to the women and booze he would be able to afford. "Like taking candy from a baby." His voice was faint but happy in tone so no one could hear him. It was all finally coming to an end, and he would have something to show for it. He did not think of the people he was going to kill, it was just another job in the long line of secret missions that he had taken over the years. He did not even think further about the man in the room that he had just left, as this meeting was such a normal occurrence in his life of espionage. All he could think about was the women and booze.

The hooded figure left in the room let out a slight snigger as he spoke. "Fool, you won't last long enough to spend what you receive. There are to be no witnesses. No survivors!" Then he was gone.

"Well, get searching. I want them captured by the end of the day!" Lance's voice sounded as anxious as he looked, as the call from his father had not come. They should have been moving hours ago but the repair had taken longer than he had hoped. This aside, it was now time to finish this chase once and for all. *This little ship we are chasing has to be close to its' last legs.*

"Captured? Sir?" Gunnery raised his voice, the sound of confusion echoing through it as he thought. *What is this fool doing?* Lance was even more of an incompetent Captain than the Gunnery had originally thought. *No matter! I will have the kill shot myself. An accident and a convenient accident at that. After all, the ship we are chasing is old and unstable.*

"You heard me, Gunnery. Get to it."

The Gunnery's answer dripped with sarcasm that he did not attempt to hide. "Yes Sir, whatever you say," however, his thoughts were now more concerned on planning how he would deliver the fatal shot to bring the criminal ship down.

Chapter 4

Two long, thin, black ears the length of two fingers end on end pricked up and out of Scrycher's pocket. The small, scale like dots covering their surface did little to protect them as the chilled air bit. As though an advanced radar, these long ears rotated through the air, scanning for sounds of danger on the landscape before them. A round head poked out of the pocket slightly, allowing its black scaly skin to be accosted by the cold air. Eyelids blinked open, revealing bold eyes as white as the snow. The eyelids rapidly blinked to protect them. The eyes were almost the size of the little creature's head, allowing him to see everything. A faint glint in the distance attracted its attention. Its head, that had followed a similar radar motion to its ears, now stopped and its beady eyes widened. The eyes did not blink, not bothering about the cold now. *Shiny!* it thought and then, in the blink of an eye, it was gone.

The black scaly creature appeared out of nowhere on the snow beside the shiny object. Its long tail, three times the length of its body, swept the snow behind it with the sharp barb on the tail's end, cutting like a knife. The creature was no bigger than a rat, with wings on its back so small that they seemed ornamental in nature. A thin, red tongue darted out suddenly to catch the shiny object in its grasp. The colour of the creature changed slightly, looking more grey, prior to disappearing again. Seconds later , it reappeared in Scrycher's pocket, carrying a shiny stone in its clawed paw. The grey colour of its scales quickly returned to black. The snow now spotting its body gave it the look of a Dalmatian, as it sat in the warm dark pocket. The little creature shook this snow from its body, spraying it into Scrycher's face.

"They'll be the death of you, Blink my boy. Those trinkets of yours!" A slight amount of humour was present in Scrycher's voice as he shook his head, and wiped the snow from his face. Blink nuzzled his hand as he purred slightly and dropped the stone into his pocket. "And I am running out of pockets." A little short-lived laugh originated from him as he continued forcing himself through the snow, one leg after the other.

Scrycher stumbled, his reactions too slow as his arms flailed. Something solid flashed before his eyes as he crashed to the ground. Wiping the snow from his face, he raised himself, catching his reflection on the jagged, frozen rock that had nearly ended his quest. He stopped to stare at himself, the bags under his eyes reminded him of his need to rest, yet the man that looked back at him was unfamiliar. His eyes welled as he saw the gruff individual he had become, his expression void of feelings, yet his eyes were deep in pain. His face blurred, others faces now replaced it in the ice, until the image settled. An innocent little boy, a smile so big on his face, now looked at him. Scrycher shook himself, then raised up, his hands forming fists as his teeth clenched and he tried to push away the tears and guilt threatening to consume him. But to no avail. "Why did you send me to the escape pods during the meteor storm? Why did I have to die? Why is Blink in your pocket and not messing in my hair?"

He fell to his knees again, shaking uncontrollably as he sobbed. "But Blink was inconsolable. He did not want to warm to me, he mourned you. He is lost without you... I am... LOST."

"We can't abandon ship yet. She won't handle much more of this." Chelsea's voice and hands shook in frustration as she worked feverishly. "I just can't get it. His location, damn it! We can't just fly blind. The Cap-"

Teller cut her off, his voice gentle, trying to calm the conversation. "It is alright. We are gaining valuable time. For every hour... minute... second... we are up here, we are giving Scrycher more time to-"

"I know, we owe it to the crew, our fallen, to hold off... But what if he is... dead." Chelsea's voice and head lowered as she finished the sentence.

Teller lifted out another belt of bullets from the crate. "I am sure if the communications were online he would be telling you to get on down there.

He is always full of surprises... Do you remember how we met, the Captain and me?" His tone, almost light and fluffy, was in stark contrast to their situation.

"You bet. You almost took his hand clean off." Chelsea laughed. She was used to this type of stress. She had been a part of Scrycher's crew for years and the rest of the crew had been together for some time. Stress had become so familiar that they often resorted to humorous conversation to get from one day to the next. This verbal outlet ultimately gave back to them that little bit of life that each one of these drawbacks and losses took away.

"Bit of an exaggeration, don't you think? I barely scratched him."

Chelsea was shocked at the response and looked up from her console for a second. "Exaggeration! You almost broke through the bars on your cell an' ripped 'im apart when you saw that crystal of yours in his hand."

"Can you blame me? The crystal is my past and my people's legacy to their children, no matter how few of us are left. I just reacted on instincts and lunged for it... with my claws extended... which was unfortunate for the Captain. I did not mean to slice his hand or chip the crystal. I still reckon it was just a little cut to his palm." Teller's voice had changed as the conversation turned to his people. His voice was sombre as he finished loading the ammunition into the Gatling gun.

"The crystal is a little more than your past now, isn't it? You forgot to mention we been using it as a compass as well! Damn, why didn't I think of that before? With the storm blockin' Scrycher's bio signs I should be searchin' for the crystals and Scrycher's combined, it'll amplify the source." Chelsea paused for a second, flicking a few controls on her panel as she mumbled to herself. "That's it, not long now, triangulate, almost there." The blips on her screen paused for a second, her fingers working on the switches again as her voice raised and she continued the conversation. "And I still can't get over how bright that crystal shone when you cut the Captain's hand and the Captain was furious. Threw the bloody thing at you covered in his blood and all." Chelsea had not taken her eyes off her workstation as she replied. She desperately searched for the Captain as the blips continued to get closer together, with the one thought still going through her mind. *I must be close.* "And Prof, he couldn't get over the way that small piece of the crystal disappeared as he was tryin' to remove it, almost as it had dissolved into the Captain's blood. That wound has still not closed up and that was months ago."

"I just wanted my crystal back. How was I to know who you were? You did kidnap me after all," he growled.

"Kidnapped you! You bloody idiot, do you, still, after all this time think that's what happened? We saved you! If we had not come when we did, you would 'ave all been captured by the Company Goons. You'd either be with the slavers or worse. You were not even conscious." Chelsea's voice had risen to make the point but now lowered as she continued. "We don't normally take adult Strays, we don't have to save you adults… Normally. You are usually powerful enough to fight your own battles, when you care to. But the children are defenceless. If we could relocate them before the Company got to them then, we were doing well."

"Why did you leave me locked up for so long then?" Teller's voice took on a questioning tone as he raised his shoulders in a gesture of confusion.

"'Cause the Boss was so pissed at you, he wanted to space you. You damn fool, the safest place for you was in the bloody brig."

Their conversation stopped abruptly as the Company vessel veered down upon them, their remaining cannon firing repeatedly at the smaller craft.

Jumping up from her station, Chelsea yelled. "Got it!" She grabbed two small memory sticks in her hand. The cannon fire hit the ship, wrenching off a shoddily welded hull plate. The ship was sent into a spin, and Chelsea to the ground. She placed the sticks between her breasts and picked herself up. Running erratically to the steering controls she tried desperately to keep her balance. No sooner than she had placed her hands on the controls, she righted the ship, pulled it one hundred-and-eighty degrees, and accelerated. During the acceleration, the ship vibrated violently, complaining about the combination of sudden movement and the first volley of cannon fire. "Now let's give 'em hell." Teller did not hear Chelsea as he was already on the

Gatling gun. Spent shells flew over the deck, the sound echoing through his head as he tried to make each shot, and every second, count...

The Gunnery's face beamed as his vessel bore down on the unsuspecting ship, his finger aggressively squeezing the trigger, activating the blazing cannons. The first of the volleys smashed into the side of the ship, wrenching one of the hull plates from it. The ship veered sideways, making it more vulnerable. *This is going to be too easy,* he thought to himself as he fired again. These thoughts were dashed as the small ship took off suddenly, manoeuvring out of the way of the second volley. The sudden movement of the ship and subsequent changes in direction were so crazy and erratic that the Gunnery was not able to predict their next movement. Thus, his sequential shots also failed to hit.

"Gunnery! Can't you just wing them so we don't have to do this all day?" The question was direct and solid as Lance stood over the Gunnery, his stare beaming down on him. The chase had become tiresome to Lance, this wounded and barely space worthy vessel was still making them look like fools.

"We have got them on the run. They can't manoeuvre like that forever, especially in that heap." The Gunnery's reply was distant as his concentration was on the fight at hand. He just kept spraying the cannon fire around the small ship, hoping for a break and hitting the small ship from time to time. These exchanges went on for what seemed an eternity. All the time the Gunnery was firing, he waited patiently for an opening. That one break he needed, at the right moment, to land the final kill shot.

Snow had covered Scrycher's thick head of hair and he appeared like an unusual snowman, now looking high in the sky yet again. *Had they survived? How had they survived? They must have survived as the fireworks in*

the sky are re-lighting the planet as they had before. His hope increased by the fact that his colleagues must still be alive, for now… His thoughts turned to their mission. The endpoint must be very close now as the crystal's light was much brighter. *If I can reach our goal, there may still be hope for us all.* Fuelled by these thoughts and a new found vitality, he started trudging again. As his pace quickened the crystal's glow increased further still. *This is no coincidence,* he thought. *The energy from above must be feeding this wondrous crystal.*

Chelsea was very good at what she did. Even though the ship was on its last legs, she had managed to get the most out of it. She was steering the ship this way and that to avoid most of the volleys of weapon fire and only taking a few hits on their damaged side.

"Get on the side we took the cannon out of. That one has not repaired itself yet, maybe we got them real good." Optimism filled Teller's voice even though he was sweating profusely, his pelt thick with sweat and sticking to his skin. His arms rippled with the obvious strain as he swung the red hot barrel of the large gun towards his target yet again.

"Still a back seat driver I see. Can't take you anywhere." Chelsea's words were full of banter but her mind was on the job.

"I'd prefer dinner, if you were going to take me anywhere. You just seem to be taking me into fire-fights. Can't say you lack excitement, though originality on the other hand…" Teller's reply was quick and decisive as the two continued their melee, their voices still holding an air of affection but neither took this situation lightly.

The Gunnery had worked out that the smaller ship was keeping to the damaged side of his vessel. *A good tactic, but not good enough.* He knew it would not be long before he could get the drop on them. With a quick glance to ensure no-one was watching, he slyly opened the red case on his weapons control panel. This revealed a switch which he flicked, using an open hand to conceal the action. Lance was none the wiser to this act of insubordination as he paced back and forth on the bridge. *Wrrrr, clunk.* The sound was lost in space as the two bay doors opened on the bottom of the vessel, unknown to all aboard except the Gunnery. The laser cannon extended out and the Gunnery input the estimated path of his target, focusing its aim at the most critical part of the unsuspecting smaller ship. His thoughts returned to those pesky criminals getting what they deserved as the laser became charged. A smirk crossed his face. *I am going to take great pleasure in this.*

Chelsea steered her small ship sideways, dodging another volley of cannon fire as the Company vessel swung around again for another pass. Their ship was breaking apart. The hull was starting to breach under the strain and part of its structure was falling around them.

"We cannot do this much longer, she will breach soon." Chelsea's voice lacked the happy banter that was common for her. "You had better get to the pods before she does."

"I am not leaving you, we are in this together." Teller had raised his voice to be heard over the gunfight, ensuring Chelsea knew how determined he was to stay.

"If I leave this station we will be shot out of the sky before we get to the pods. We will be sitting ducks!" A tear rolled down Chelsea's cheek as she knew there was now no hope for her, and, possibly not even Teller.

"Turn the ship into the planet, Chelsea!"

"Why, Teller?"

"Just do it woman, and do it now!"

Chelsea quickly forced the steering stick forward and to the side, throwing the ship into one last sharp turn towards the planet. The manoeuvre was perfectly executed but too late. A laser shot smashed into the hull causing a massive breach in the middle of the cockpit with the compartment they were in de-pressurising quickly as the air was sucked from it.

Teller leapt effortlessly out of his gun pod, his body becoming a blur as he hit the deck and scrambled on all fours. Teller's shoulder smashed into Chelsea, cracking her ribs and winding her, guiding her over his shoulder in the same forceful motion; the impact knocking one of the memory sticks from her breasts. Chelsea barely caught it between two fingers before she allowed herself to relax slightly and an intense pain shot through her chest. They had only just made it out the cabin as the blast door shut. The cockpit was now shut off completely, stopping the rest of the ship from becoming de-pressurised. But this action also stopped them from controlling the ship.

The firing had stopped outside as the little ship started spiralling out of control. The Company vessel obviously knew they were done for. Chelsea had not had time to put the automatic pilot on. The pilot's stick had fallen forward, dragging them towards the planet's atmosphere to a certain grave. The spinning motion of the ship did not affect Teller as he continued bounding, never stopping, using his two legs and his free arm to increase his speed. He raced for the pods knowing it was their only hope of survival. There was no way Chelsea could have made it to them in time, or even kept her balance long enough to get moving. However, Teller was like a panther, pouncing from one obstacle to another, all the time moving forward to his destination. Chelsea knew what Teller was capable of. He was the fastest, strongest Stray she had ever seen, so she allowed him to cradle her on his shoulder, their lives now in his hands.

The ship was spiralling out of control, the floors twisting and turning, and furniture being flung from one part of the ship to another, smashing into pieces on impact with the inner hull. Teller's long claws ripped into the ribbed decking, causing blood to ooze from their joints as the pressure of his sprint tore them partially from his flesh. The gun chambers were thrown open as their rusty hinges and padlocks were broken by the strain of the ship's constant, yet erratic, motion. Ammunition and weapons were flung around the room randomly. Teller's quick reflexes allowed him to drop to dodge an incoming rifle. He dropped forward onto his free hand and Chelsea's head hit the deck with a thud as a shotgun smashed into her shoulder. The movement was just enough to avoid the shotgun himself and a direct hit to his head that would have ended their desperate escape.

Teller paused momentarily, concerned about the bashing Chelsea was taking. This pause lasted a split second as he leapt again. He knew he could not slow down as the ship was spinning more erratically. He was thankful for the meshing design of the ship as his claws were able to rip through it and grip between each step or leap; and his claws were grasping whatever came under them, be it floor, wall, ceiling or furniture.

As he tore open the double doors to the galley, the ship lurched. His grip on the steel curved handle was so tight his fingers turned white as he held on for dear life. Teller dodged the cans and utensils that flew through the door. Using the door as a shield, he managed to protect them from being skewered by the many knives flying by. Seconds later, these utensils were piercing the steel lockers doors and the walls behind them. As his strong muscular arms swung Chelsea and himself up through the doorway, the ship lurched again. This time levelling slightly, allowing him to use this moment to get quickly into the next room. He had moved too fast to see the danger as a small frying pan smashed into Chelsea's cheek, her cheek and face instantly black and swollen. Chelsea lent sideways, spitting out blood as her aching body heaved for breath.

"This is fun, Teller." She managed to wince out. "Just like a joy ride." The joke doing little to cover the pain.

Teller did not hear her speak as he was too focused. The dining table in the centre of the room, thankfully attached to the floor, was his next target. He leapt, his claws ripping into the steel framework of the table as he landed. He levered himself into an optimal position for another leap to the other side of the room, this preparation essential for conserving his energy for the escape to succeed.

The ship lurched suddenly as it hit the atmosphere; it was past creaking and roared like a wounded animal, its hull crumpling like a tin can. A large frying pan had levered off its hook in the pantry, the pantry door was missing, joining the flying debris that had removed it. The momentum of the ship sent the pan flying into Teller's chest. He faltered but the pain did not register as a gash opened in his chest, splattering blood over the table. He strengthened his grip on the table and Chelsea, as the ship straightened further. It was in an almost level sideways position, causing its descent to slow. One magnificent leap sent them through the open door on the other side of the room, this doorway leading into the brig. Teller took advantage of the rusty bars of the cells, swinging from one to the next using only a single arm to swing. The hand holding Chelsea was only letting her go to grasp the bar before it. He resembled a monkey, travelling through trees, and this quick thinking hastened their escape.

Chelsea was trying to be as limp as possible in order to ensure him more freedom of movement. However, her pain was increasing and her body was working against her, tensing at each movement.

The ship lurched again as its wing cracked, straining under the pressure of the uncontrolled descent. Personal items assailed them as Teller flew across the crew quarters; lamps, books and clothes all falling onto them as well as smaller items that were easily avoided by his quick and nimble movement.

He gripped the walls with his digits, his claws outstretched and still cutting into the steel of the ship. Blood was dripping from some of these as several of the claws were missing, left in the decks or furniture at previous stages of his escape. This seemed not to worry him in the slightest, as the adrenaline continued to keep the pain away. Leaping from steel bed to steel bed, he grew anxious. They were almost at the pods with barely a few metres more to their goal. He grabbed the hatch door and threw it open, slinging Chelsea's body inside. Her aching body hit the hard floor with a thud, but at least she was alive.

The ship creaked violently, lurching sideways as the wing was now ripped off. The kitchen and weapon lockers were the first items sucked out of the huge breach and the rest of the ship was soon to follow suit, ripping itself apart with the structural integrity faulting. Teller envisioned himself being sucked out with the rest of the items, but the blast doors on the prison cells closed; blocking him from imminent death. He relaxed to allow his body to stoop, the ship lurching violently as he tried to swing himself into the pod. Straps holding the crates of merchandise in the cargo bay started giving way, splitting slowly. Another sudden lurch of the ship caused the straps to snap, allowing the buckles to fly out of control. They travelled through the plastic curtains, one of them smashing into the hull to the left of Teller, leaving a large dent from the impact. Relieved that it had not hit him, he lent forward, feeding his head into the pod. The crates were thrown from their position by another huge lurch of the ship as the second wing ripped off. This time the crates were thrown clear of the racking as there were no straps to hold them. They crashed through the makeshift curtains and out of the cargo room. One crate slammed into Teller's back, its edge crashing into him. His body followed the momentum pummelling him into the pod, his head slamming into the metal inside. This final impact was too much for his battered body to take, and he lost consciousness.

A barely coherent Chelsea regained some sense of purpose, manoeuvring Teller's limp arm inside the pod. She reached over his unconscious body, pulling the lever. With this action, the door to the pod closed and it jettisoned. *Hisss, thump.* Chelsea sighed in relief at the sound, only to cringe at the painful effort of it. The panel on the wall lit up as they aimlessly continued behind the ship in its descent to the planet. Chelsea pulled one of the memory cards from her bosom inserting it in this panel, it in turn lit up. The panel recognised the data as descent patterns and activated them. Chelsea laid back uncomfortably, their coordinates to the Capitan now set.

The pod's tiny engines fired, attempting to send it to its new location. It had almost made its adjustments when debris from the falling ship smashed into one of the engines, sending the pod spinning out of control. The bodies were bounced around aggressively inside it before the air cushions expanded, allowing barely enough room for them to breathe as the pod spun to the planet below.

The Gunnery smiled from ear to ear as the ship went down. He had done his job, and the laser had done its by ripping through the cockpit section of the small ship. As no one could possibly have survived the quick de-pressurisation of the cockpit, his thoughts quickly returned to the promised payment. He thought of spending it on the beer wenches, easy living, silk clothes, all so he could have the easy life he had always wanted. *No more hauling around the stars cleaning up the trash.* He fondled his controls as he thought of this. These thoughts were rudely interrupted.

"What did I say, Gunnery? You incompetent fool! Wound them!" Lance was fuming. His face was bright red with anger, his nose raised, mouth slightly open and teeth bared.

The Gunnery looked up at the figure in front of him. *So he does have some balls*, he thought, *a little too late though*. He had done his job and Lance's orders had not mattered. The Gunnery just smirked at the Captain. *Whatever.*

During this heated exchange, neither man had seen the pod. Nor the mechanical arms holding it as they stretched out, only to be ripped apart prior to releasing it from the crumpling wreck of the ship. Or when the small engines on the escape pod cut in, directing it to the destination that had now been input into its controls.

"Captain ... Captain."

Lance's gaze had not left the Gunnery. "When we get back, I will see you removed from this ship!" Lance was scolding him.

Rightly so, the Gunnery smirked, his retirement still on his mind.

"Captain! Captain!" The voice repeated its plea with more emphasis.

"What is it, man?" Lance turned and out of the corner of his eye caught the movement of something small in the wake of the ship's debris, now plummeting to the planet below. His mood calmed a little and the redness drained from his face as it was replaced with pale white and an expression of shock. "How the?" *This crew were good.* Lance knew the layout of the ship they were attacking, and no one should have escaped that wreckage. There just had not been enough time for anyone to get to those escape pods if they were all in the cockpit.

The Gunnery realised what was happening and his thoughts of wenches and wine were dispelled from his head. He grabbed his cannon controls. Desperately he sent a volley of cannon fire towards the escape pod. With the cannon fire not reaching the target, the Gunnery; desperation plastered across his face, turned his attention back to the laser. *Click, Click, Click, Click, Click.* Nothing happened.

"You fool! You used up all our power. The laser has only one shot." Lance's face returned to blood red as his nostrils flared.

The escape pod's descent was too fast, they both knew they would not be able to hit it now. *Why had both men been too pre occupied by bickering like children?* They turned to each other with their jaws now dropped, *what had they done?* Neither saw the pod getting smashed with debris from the ship nor one of its engines being damaged so it was now unable to control its own descent. The pod was plummeting aimlessly to the planet below, the crash of the pod and deaths of both inside, imminent…

Chapter 5

Scrycher watched the fireworks in the sky, this time more magnificent than the last. He knew this could only mean that the fight between the two ships would have to be much closer to the planet. Light from the fire-fight spread above them in a dome of red beauty. The crystal in his left hand grew brighter as it continued to absorb more of the energy that was being amplified in the atmosphere. Scrycher's optimism returned as he spoke softly, not wanting to jinx the situation. "They must have survived, I knew they would not go down that easy."

A blinding flash of white light filled the air, the light so intense it could only mean one thing. The Company vessel's Captain had resorted to using the laser. Scrycher's heart sank in his chest just as quickly as his hope had been restored moments earlier, his stomach now in knots. Scrycher's attention was diverted from his feeling of dread to the crystal as it responded again to the new form of light. The crystal now gave off a solid stream of bright light, shining into the distance, so bright that Scrycher winced; his eyes hurting as he looked at it. He followed it through the falling snow, confirming the direction of his goal. His final destination was now very obvious as a halo encircled what appeared to be a large cavern entrance, set in a huge mountain in the distance.

Scrycher's attention was drawn from the cave as a red glow started emanating above them, getting brighter and brighter. As the light got closer to them, the whole planet started to glow a magnificent red, intensifying as it reflected off the snow. His heart stopped beating momentarily, he knew this would be his ship. The sheer bulk of the Company vessel would have been visible by now if it were falling from space. His little ship's wreck made its way into the atmosphere like a sun, falling out of the sky, with a red tail as far as the eye could see.

Scrycher stood watching the wreck as it plummeted down through the atmosphere. He knew he had to get moving as it was headed straight for his location. His attention was diverted from his thoughts of fleeing as his left hand started tingling. This tingling turned to discomfort as the crystal's glow turned to heat. The hot glow originating from the crystal soon became so intense it started to burn. He juggled the crystal, swapping it to his right hand. The hand that Teller had wounded at the start of this journey; which still had not healed.

The crystal took advantage of this open wound, getting inside the one it had started changing before. It had been interrupted those three months ago but now it had the opportunity to finish its transformation. As the crystal touched the blood on Scrycher's hand, it inserted much of its life force into him in one steady flow. His hand clenched in response to the invasion of his body by this foreign force. All his muscles tightened as the crystal forced its energy into the wound, his muscles so contracted he was unable to let it go as his body arched in an attempt to break free. Power continued surging into his body, dropping him to his knees. The unbearable pain forced him to the ground, as it burnt through his blood, working its way to his veins to finally follow them to his heart. The white energy changed his heart physically and chemically, its genes being re-written so that it could absorb the energy. His heart's strength increased, allowing it to pump quicker and with much less effort, sending the new found power quickly to the rest of his body. Doing this, it spread, as though a disease consuming him. Changing him, like it had his heart, as it travelled to every inch of his being.

Blink huddled fearfully in Scrycher's pocket, unsure of what was happening to his new master. To this little dragon, Scrycher's appearance was that of someone having a heart attack.

Scrycher dropped sideways as he clutched his arm, his eyes still open, unable to move and the fear consumed him. He did not know what was happening to him, but he did know that a great ball of fire was headed towards them. Laying there horrified, he watched, unable to do anything. His senses were still keen, and he could hear the howling of the wind and wild animals he had not heard until now. It was obvious that they too sensed the change in temperature and the incoming catastrophe. What animals lived on the unforgiving planet he did not know. He had seen tracks but no form of life and he hoped he would not find out. All he knew for sure was that something was living on this barren wasteland of snow and ice. There he was, paralysed, unable to move, and unable to defend himself if the need arose. He drew little comfort in knowing that the animals, if they did come for him, would not have time to feed on his flesh. The ship plummeting straight for him would crush him before it burnt his flesh from his bones and anything that was near.

The mangled vessel hurtled through the atmosphere with its bulk burning intensely. With its structure all but gone, it resembled nothing of its former self, appearing in the sky above as a melted wreck of burning metal. Scrycher, still incapacitated, lay in the snow. He could smell the burning as the heat attacked his nostrils. The smell almost made him sick, if he could be sick. He was still frozen in pain. His body had not yet finished changing, the power continuing to make its way through him, producing a glow under his skin. The landscape illuminated in this same glow as the snow seemed to get brighter, glowing iridescently, seemingly absorbing the light raining down upon it in the same fashion as the crystal was absorbing the power and then expelling it.

All the power that the snow and land exuded did not matter as the ship was still heading straight towards Scrycher. The planet could do nothing to change the outcome, or could it? The ship's descent slowed, its burning still intense. Its original course changed as if though it had hit something or was redirected by an unknown force away from Scrycher. It seemed as though the planet wanted him alive after all. Maybe he would survive this ordeal. The vessel continued on its deflected course, crashing into the snowy mountains he had just travelled between. The impact of the collision threw up chunks of rocks, dust particles and snow in all directions. Much of the landscape had been dispersed, melted, or fused in the intense heat. Soil and rock lay exposed; many of these rocks harboured small crystals, some darkened by the burning heat, but all of them sparkled in the radius of the fire; reflecting its heat and absorbing its power. The unmasked crystals glowed brighter with each passing second as the air around them became one big power source.

Scrycher heard and felt, but could not see this unfolding as he was facing the other direction. The direction the ship had come from and where his destination lay. The pod broke through the atmosphere, visible only now as it was out of the tail of its mother ship. This Scrycher could see. *Not again!* The pod was also heading directly towards him. It entered the atmosphere with its hull still intact, but its descent was way too fast. The occupants would not survive; they would be crushed on impact. The only comfort to Scrycher was that he knew their lifeless bodies would be protected from the elements and the wild animals. Their bodies would soon be encased in a metal tomb.

Scrycher wished he could close his eyes, not wanting to watch such a horrific crash. He watched as debris impacted the snow around him, barely missing his body. Fear gripped him as a chunk of the pod, its anchoring arm, crashed by his head. Snow dispersed, the ground shook, he could feel the heat from the debris burning at his flesh, but he could still not move. It was not his fear that held him but the crystal in his hand, controlling his body, still not letting him move. The crystal glow intensified further as it continued to funnel its energy into Scrycher. It continued to burn through his body like the fires around him, until it reached his brain. The pain, the unbearable fear; it was all too much for his human body to take. Scrycher's breathing quickened, trying to expel this power; but it was too late. His head rolled into the snow as he lost consciousness…

Scrycher watched as the pod's descent suddenly slowed and it levelled out to land with a light "thud" in the snow. The snow acted like a pillow, cushioning the pod as it touched the ground. The immediate danger over, the pod allowed the air cushions inside it to be released. The battered occupants gained more space to move, allowing them to sleep more comfortably and to recover from this ordeal. Scrycher felt himself looking at the land below as he travelled quickly

along the snow to find a cavern. A cavern, which he entered. He continued through the tunnels, a hundred red eyes watching him, to finally glide to a glowing crystal shield. He touched the shield; it glimmered then pulsed, letting him through. He entered a room to finally lay at the bottom of a huge crystalline tree. The light in the tree, similar to that of the crystal, was dimming; dimming into nothing. The tree was exhausted by this ordeal. All of the tree's life force that was left was now directed to the barely lit capsules around the room. Looking, he could see a capsule beneath the tree, housing him, comforting him, beckoning him...

The crystal's intense glow diminished as it stopped transferring its energy into Scrycher's body. Its work was now complete. It had changed this one called Scrycher as it had many before him. The crystal had thought that Scrycher was like the others, the ones lost long ago from this place, so it had changed him like it had done them. Given him the power. It had given to him energy that it had given to the others and it had been absorbed easily into his body. His body and mind had been an open book in his time of grief, hungry for the power and the change. The crystal had made Scrycher's body and mind strong, enabling it to receive the energy freely, without damaging it. This should have been all that was required. The change was all that was required in the past. But, the change was not all that was required now! This one was different! The crystal had not encountered one like this before, in its years, centuries, of changing. The crystal dwelled on its mistake for a second, sending itself into him. The light diminished from the crystal briefly, relighting as it re-emerged out of Scrycher and back into its shell. It knew now that its energy was absorbed by Scrycher, and the change was definitely complete. The crystal was sure of that, but the change was still wrong and it did not know why...

It thought to itself. The energy was being amplified as it had been with all the others. This was a given as Scrycher's structure was perfect for the task. But the energy was not being expelled! This expelling of energy was what the crystal and the planet required to continue their existence in this delicate circle of life. Instead of releasing this energy, this vessel called Scrycher somehow stored the energy, the same way the crystal did, only using it differently. This vessel was keeping the energy for its own selfish purpose, not sharing and not giving back to the cycle of life.

The crystal knew that the life of the planet, and the crystal was all that should have mattered. To this end, this energy, the energy stored inside Scrycher, needed to go somewhere but it could not find a way out. Scrycher's breathing quickened as his body desperately attempted to find a way to expel this energy. This did not work! The energy overloaded Scrycher's body, making it shut down as if an emergency stop was pushed, allowing his body to sleep; to try to repair itself in slumber. Scrycher's body was partially correct, as the crystal knew. Scrycher would not absorb power in time of sleep so he was safe. For now…

"Take your crew down to the surface, and ensure you finish the job this time!" Lord Dragoon's voice was strong and decisive, marginally below yelling.

"But Father, I did as you asked. The ship is destroyed." Lance had definitely had enough of the chase now. He just wanted to go home, to leave this place, and his voice was betraying this to his father. "We scanned the planet. There is no sun. No warmth. Only snow! How could anyone possibly survive down there?" He did not want to go down to this cold planet. He was not about to leave the comforts of his ship to chase these criminals, all because the Gunnery Sergeant could not control himself. How the Gunnery could not follow a simple order, Lance did not know.

"You have said yourself, you cannot control your crew, so stop being a whimpering fool and get them all down there, including that useless Gunnery of yours! Take all your men and do not return until you have done your job!" His father's image blinked off the screen, leaving Lance in the room alone to ponder what to do next. *Maybe I should start by finding that bloody Gunnery Sergeant.*

"Gunnery, you failed me! They still live…"

"But it was a fluke. They should never have survived to make it to the pods. I hit them dead in the cockpit area." The Gunnery's voice was nervous. He so wanted this to be over and to collect his payment.

"You will be given another chance shortly. I have arranged it. Make sure you do not fail me further." The hooded figure's voice was emotionless.

"But I destroyed the ship as you ordered and no-one could survive in that extreme, cold environment. I ran the scans myself and they would last maybe a few days at most down on the planet before they died from the cold." The Gunnery had the same opinion as Lance. He did not want to go down to that inhospitable planet if he did not have too.

"We cannot take any chances. All of the criminals must be dead before you leave that planet." The cloaked figure raised his voice, knowing these six words would get him what he wanted. "Or you will not receive payment!"

"Yes, Sir." Gunnery left, swearing under his breath. He had to do this thing, otherwise the last three months of sabotaging Lance's command was for nothing.

A crooked smile appeared under the hood of the man left in the room. "Not long now and I will have everything I need." Then he was gone…

Chapter 6

The Snow Leopard's paws sank slightly into the snow under the weight of his large mass as it crept around Scrycher. Hungry for its next meal, he was cautiously observing his prey, waiting for the right moment to make the kill.

Blink had feverishly worked his way out of Scrycher's pocket. It had taken some time and effort as the pocket was full of trinkets, so he was looking forward to sitting on Scrycher's chest. This was not to be. At the sight of danger, Blink had extended his back fin, screeching like a frightened bird as he tried to make himself look more menacing. He instead looked very insignificant as he tried to guard Scrycher and ward off this large beast.

The Leopard continued circling its prey, not threatened by the attempted distraction. He was after a feast, not a snack. The Leopard made its move, darting in and grabbing Scrycher's hand. The crystal touched the Leopard briefly and transferred its essence into the creature before falling to the snow. This mere touch was enough to start the change! The Leopard's fangs pierced the soft wound on Scrycher's hand, oblivious to the change that had now started inside its own blood.

Blink lurched forward with fangs barred.

The Leopard took notice of Blink this time, growling a menacing warning as it pawed at him. It looked up with its bold eyes; *this little creature might be a threat after all.* Blink screeched, backing away from the Leopard's reach, but stayed crouched protectively on Scrycher.

This was a much better feast than the Leopard was used to. He was not about to let this pesky little creature stop it from getting the meal back to its lair and its kittens, awaiting a feed of fresh kill. The Leopard started dragging the body along the cold snow leaving a small ditch in its path.

Every muscle in its upper body tensed with the strain. The Leopard could feel the warm blood on its tongue. The blood was strange; powerful! The power in Scrycher's blood found a release. It expelled itself through this new wound, coursing through the Leopard's body. The crystal had already done its part on the Leopard and now the energy started working, changing the Leopard as it had Scrycher. The transformation occurred quickly. This creature was much less complex to change as its body was native to the planet. The change was still only partially completed as the Leopard released its hold on Scrycher's hand. He could not eat this one, this one's purpose was too important! The Leopard's coat glowed, expelling the energy into the atmosphere, warming the air around it. The Leopard watched Scrycher, as he skulked away to find somewhere to let the transformation complete itself. The tension in Scrycher's body eased a little, then his breathing returned to normal. The excess power was expelled from his body and had transferred to this animal, potentially saving his life!

Scrycher fumbled with the latch. His hands were cold again, numb, and the hatch to the pod was stuck. Cursing, he jammed his foot on the pod, pulling at the latch with all his might. His muscles started rippling and a vein became apparent on his forehead, as the strain became too much. He gave one last pull, the last of his energy used in one movement. *Clunk*, the latch came free, his grasp came free too. Losing his balance, his bum bounced on the snow, and he cursed again as a stench of vomit exploded from the pod.

As he rolled in his slumber, Teller sensed the warmth above him. Instinctively his arm stretched out, curving his wrist intimately cradling her head, allowing him to take the weight of her body as it fell. Chelsea's feet hit the ground first then he gently lowered her body and head. He awoke to extreme pain shooting through his back and shoulder. Realising he was cradling Chelsea's limp body in his arm, he completed the act of gently lowering her over the entrance of the life pod, into the soft cold snow below.

Blink who had returned to Scrycher's pocket, was messing with a small fragment of shiny hull. At the sudden movement of Scrycher falling to the ground, the little creature lifted his head, his scales rising to a defensive position. He looked around, noticing that Scrycher had just fallen and there was no danger. He lowered his defences slightly but left his scales shackled as he gurgled and shook his head in a disapproving manner, scolding Scrycher for being so careless. Seeing no other apparent danger, and knowing Scrycher was adequately told off, he dropped his aggressive guard, and went back to fiddling with his shiny object.

With the pod finally open, and Blink occupied, Scrycher could see inside. The bodies of Chelsea, and Teller, lay inside the pod, unconscious or sleeping. Scrycher observed this from his sitting position in the snow, his pride hurt; especially after the scolding from Blink. He watched in amazement as Teller's reactions allowed him to gently lower Chelsea as she fell off his body, and out of the pod, softly guided into the snow below.

Teller looked up to see Scrycher observing him from the sitting position.

"Smooth move, Teller, I can see why she is sweet on you." The embarrassment left Scrycher, as he welcomed his friend in his own subtle way.

Teller blushed, the redness barely visible through all the bruising. "We did not think we would make it." Looking at Chelsea's bruised and battered body he replied as his eyes started weeping. The shock of the whole ordeal was just too much for him to keep his emotions in check.

"What did you do to my bloody ship? It's in pieces all over the planet. How am I supposed to carry your lazy arse around the galaxy now? On my back?"

Teller looked at Scrycher trying to gauge his expression. "How are you supposed to carry me on your back when you can't even stand up?" He smirked ever so slightly, barely apparent under all the facial bruising. "Um, and I was in a bit of a hurry to get off the ship, sorry, forgot to put it on Auto Pilot."

"Well you did, did you? Bloody silly thing that." Scrycher let a small smile come over his face, allowing Teller to ease his troubled expression.

"We are all here now and that is all that matters. How is she?" Scrycher stood up awkwardly as the fall had hurt more than his pride. Gingerly he walked over to Chelsea and bent down, smoothing his hand over her forehead, or what resembled a forehead through all the bruises and swelling.

"She could be worse Captain, we had a big complication..."

"Please explain?"

"Something's changed. The Company vessel went for the kill shot. They did not attempt to wound our ship, just stun us long enough to go for the kill. They used the laser. It ripped through the cockpit while we were both in there. It was all that I could do, just to get us out alive. I don't think they want us alive any more." Teller moved his aching body awkwardly out of the pod as he spoke. Scrycher gave him a hand to get out. They resembled two little old men the way they both were nursing their aching bodies.

"The Company ship will be here soon, so we had better get moving." Scrycher was looking into the sky with a worried expression on his face as he searched for signs of a descending vessel.

"What are we going to do about Chelsea? I can't carry her without hurting her further." A look of concern was obvious in Teller's eyes as he looked over Chelsea's broken body.

Scrycher reached into the pod pulling on a latch in the ceiling. A small packet dropped out which he opened revealing several large syringes. He took out one of these syringes making sure it was full and very carefully stuck the needle in Chelsea's neck. He pushed on the end of the syringe so the clear liquid entered her blood. Chelsea's body seemed to immediately relax, as much as a battered body could. He checked her over once more, her body still, except for the erratic movement of her chest. Looking up, he replied to the unspoken question. "It is an illegal pain killer, one that should calm her body, allowing it to heal faster." He allowed himself to smile a little again as he wrapped the remainder of the syringes back up in the packet. "One of the perks of the job!"

Scrycher crawled into the pod. Once in, he tried pulling off a side panel. It was stuck, the latch broken in the collision with Teller's head. Teller leant back into the pod and together they yanked at the latch. This time the latch came loose, sending Teller sprawling to the soft, snow covered ground.

Blink's eyes lit up as a small gurgle came from his throat. Scrycher allowed himself a little smile as the stretcher that had been in the compartment fell onto him.

"This is no time for sitting on your bum, Teller. Give me a hand with this thing." Teller raised himself off the ground, grabbing the stretcher as Scrycher fed it out of the pod. "Well. Let's get to it. The Company won't wait all day for us to get a head start." Scrycher's old bantering mood had returned, for now.

Carefully they moved Chelsea's body onto the stretcher. She was in much worse shape than either of them had thought, with her whole body grazed, bruised and swollen. Scrycher reached into his pocket, pulling out the crystal that he had carried as a compass on the planet. He passed this crystal in a very ceremonial way to Teller. "Show us the way… Mr Story Teller."

Teller smiled, placing the glowing crystal on Chelsea's chest. Picking up either end of the stretcher, they started to trudge off, following the bright beam originating from the crystal. Scrycher looked towards their destination of the large cave as they started walking, with Teller taking the lead. As he scanned the landscape, he noticed a large welt on Teller's back even through the cloak. *What hell they must have gone through*, he thought. *They were lucky to escape with their lives.* The two men trudged through the snow, their goal driving them to their unknown destination with the weight of the stretcher barely felt by either man.

Blink was very proud of himself. With head cocked and tail in the air, he took a guarding position on this stretcher. He was making sure no one took them unawares. He would be there to protect them all. He was strutting up and down the length of the stretcher when a howl from the Leopard boomed through the air, the transformation in the beast complete. Blink stopped his pacing immediately and dropped onto his belly, his paws automatically covering his eyes, while his body shivered uncontrollably. His shivering body rattled the stretcher momentarily until he blinked into Scrycher's pocket. Scrycher laughed, as did Teller.

"It is alright, Blink. We all get scared!"

Chapter 7

"What do you think is doing this to us Teller? Making us feel so good that is."

Travelling in the snow was hard, and both Teller's and Scrycher's bodies now ached, however, not in the way they should have. Neither of the men was cold, even though it had started snowing heavily, making it near impossible to see a few metres in front of them. Somehow, in the three days of travelling, the wounds on Teller's body had healed. The large welt on his back had completely gone, and his fur was glowing, and, odder still, the air around him was warming. The glow of his coat was so intense it was visible even through the large black cloak that he wore. Teller's eyes, which were normally jet black, had also gained lustre. Both men felt better than they had for years. It was as though the crystal, this planet, was rejuvenating them. Although Teller's wounds had almost completely healed, Scrycher's hand had not. Scrycher was not concerned, as the feeling in the rest of his body well and truly made up for it.

"Not sure, but I think it has something to do with the life cycle on this planet. In all the visions the crystal showed there seemed to be a glow, one from the Strays and a similar glow from the crystals, be it a crystal tree or the grass. I believe this to be that planet, our planet, our ancestor's home!" Teller sounded fascinated by the way the world seemed to be working.

"It does not seem to be having the same effect on Chelsea, though. She is healing very slowly, and I am running out of drugs. Any suggestions?" Scrycher's voice showed the concern as well as the look on his face. Chelsea was healing, but it was not fast enough. Soon the drugs would be gone, and there would only be pain for her. Then she really would be dead weight, the pain would be intoxicating to her and in a fight, dead weight was as good as dead.

"I believe, as we are both Stray descendants, this planet can somehow affect us. It seems to affect me more than you as I am pure blood. Chelsea is pure human with no inbreeding. She is as foreign to this planet as the Company was two thousand years ago."

The two men rounded a ridge. They stood in awe at the sight of the entrance to a cave. The caverns mountain was maybe a half day's travel but twice the height of any other structure in the surrounding area, and five times as wide, its colossal size dwarfing everything in the landscape around it. The landscape had changed considerably. The ground was no longer flat, there were cliffs and mountains all around, but none like the mountain cave that now towered before them. The crystal was still resting on Chelsea with its brightness amplified and its ray of light projecting straight into the cave. With added intensity the light from the crystal shone, their compass was now pointing out what they thought to be their final destination. Teller turned to Scrycher who was already looking at him. They paused, neither of them speaking. Their eyes started welling up as the culmination of the three months seemed to be finally coming to an end, filling both men's hearts with new hope.

"We've found it. At long last. We've found it!" Teller's voice was yelling as he dropped to his knees, resting the stretcher in the soft snow.

He looked up at Scrycher who was now facing in the opposite direction to watch a small shuttle descending. It was but a dot in the distance but their keen eyes that had been amplified by the power could see it.

"And they have found us…"

It had been three days since they had blown the small ship out of the sky. Lance had waited to venture to the planet in the hope that the criminals they were following had either perished in the landing, or, in the cold of the following days. He had not, and still did not want, conflict or the shedding of blood. Lance thought that waiting to see if they perished on their own in this harsh landscape seemed like the easiest action to take.

Therefore, this was the course he took, much to the dismay of the crew. The crew was growing restless so when they had found no bodies in the wreckage of the pod, it had not gone down at all well. The very faint tracks formed in the bare mud leading away from it, maybe days old, just added to the resentment of his crew. This simple decision so right at the time now seemed so wrong, turning what should have been a simple capture into a hunt. The thought of the hunt was daunting to all in this unforgiving landscape of rocks, hills and caves that could easily allow the criminals many opportunities to ambush the small Company crew.

"Captain Dragoon, as your first plan did not work out so well, I believe we should follow mine. After all, I am the senior military man in this command."

The Commander's plan was simple: land as far enough away from the criminals so as for them not to see their shuttle coming, then launch an assault. Capture if possible, kill if not. He preferred killing but capture was acceptable. Capture was only an option in his mind as he had come to admire the crew of the small ship; a crew that could out think and outdistance a Company vessel, even if they were mere criminals and this vessel commanded by an incompetent Captain like Lance. The Commander cocked his rifle to show that he was ready as Lance looked up.

"Certainly Commander! I would not want to cramp your style."

Teller sat on the ledge that the two men had decided to set up as a sentry point. They took turns so that it was guarded at all times, and the Company could not sneak up on them. As Teller watched, his thoughts returned to Chelsea. She had recovered slightly over these last few days, the warmth of the cave helping her body heal. She was still unconscious, but she was definitely on the mend. His only concern was that they were down to their last syringe of drugs. With this gone, her body would have all the pain of her injuries, and no relief from it. Teller's body had no such problem, the strange light illuminating from it warmed the air around him as he sat there. The snow melting before it was able to land on his cloak.

The snow was not the only thing that was landing. Teller's eyes squinted, looking into the distance at the shuttle as its thrusters blew all the snow from the ground around it, landing softly, and scorching the ground. Teller watched as one man exited the shuttle, then another. Shortly later, another seven more men exited, one after the other, all tiny, appearing as if ants, in the distance. Teller's heart quickened as he jumped down from the vantage point above the cave entrance, landing elegantly on all fours in front of the cave. Standing, his thoughts turned to the nine men that had landed, the men coming to hunt them like animals. As he thought of these things, he turned towards Scrycher inside the cave. "They have landed, just past the third hill. What are we to do now? You know they will kill us if they find us."

Scrycher was cleaning his rifle, the cloth that had wrapped the syringes coming in handy. The last syringe sat on a ledge in the cave wall. Scrycher was making sure that the chamber of his rifle would not jam during this fight. He handled it as though handling a lover, caressing it up and down. "I am not going to wait in here for them to corner and butcher us like animals. We will have to up the stakes! We play to win, no more worrying about killing anyone. Are you up to it?" Scrycher's voice was very stern and his facial expression the most serious Teller had ever seen.

Teller looked into the small fire they had prepared in the cave and then at Chelsea, her body recovering, but still badly damaged. "I suppose I will have to be, under the circumstances. We have no other choice, do we?" Teller was looking for a way out of bloodshed, as he never liked it much. He preferred the role of negotiator but that time had passed. This was all portrayed in the sombre tone of his voice.

"Well, we will have lots of time to get out there and prepare, they would be counting on the element of their surprise. They do not know we have a vantage point to see them land. I would put them a day away, possibly more as it took us a day and a half to get from that point to here." Scrycher had finished cleaning his rifle and had extended the blade from its butt, now polishing the razor sharp blade on his sleeve. "No rush!" He eyed the blade as the fire's reflection enhanced its beauty and he spoke gently, "you will taste blood soon enough."

The small shuttle came in for its landing, with its thrusters at full power, to allow it to land quietly; the heat from them was so intense it melted the snow and scorched the ground around the vessel. The quiet approach was necessary if they were to take the criminals by surprise. Lance knew this, but he did not have to be happy with the half day trek required to get them to their destination through the snow covered land. The cave, where the criminals were possibly hauled up and taking refuge from the elements, looked so far away, and unreachable.

Wiiiiirrrrrrrrrrrr. The shuttle door opened quickly, its length providing the steps in and out of the shuttle. Gunnery was the first to walk out as he was anxious to get this over and done with. The payment for killing these criminals was the only thing on his mind. The quicker they were killed, the sooner he could start spending. His thoughts of the payment were quickly replaced by the burning of the cold air assailing his nostrils. *How could anyone survive this?* He thought. He had not been on a mission like this for years; the seven military men still on board ensured this. They did not like others getting 'in their way'. The hooded figure must have really had some power to get him on this mission…

As Lance exited the shuttle, his boot sloshed in the melted snow. He looked down to the side of the ramp where the snow had melted clear, like pure water. Lance had not seen pure water before, just the brown sludge that was recycled on the stations and ships of the Company. Kneeling down on a patch of snow, he faltered slightly as the cold worked its way through his pants, wetting them. Regaining his composure, he cupped his hands and leant forward to place them into the water. To his amazement, both hands were still visible in the crystal clear water. Lance looked at his hands for a moment then he lifted a handful of water up to his face as he pursed his lips. The water tingled on his lips and its taste was indescribable, so pure and untainted. He wondered if this was why his father had been so concerned about this planet. It was covered in snow the whole way around, and would be worth half the Company's wealth, easily making whomever controlled it very rich and powerful indeed…

The Commander, an elderly man, spoke to his men in a stern and direct tone. With an upright stance and head raised; he radiated a no nonsense attitude. "We know they have not perished thus far as there are no bodies, only wreckage. We have seen a couple of tracks barely visible further on. We are assuming these are from the criminals we are to apprehend." They had established this from the air as the shuttle had come in for landing. "We are on a capture mission as per Captain Dragoon's orders, but our safety comes first. If it comes down to it; shoot first, ask questions later!"

The six soldiers looked at each other, then at the Commander. The Commander's glare told them in no uncertain terms that he wanted no questions.

"Right on, Commander!" They all spoke in unison, then filed out of the shuttle in single file and in one smooth movement.

The nine men had been travelling for the better part of a day. They were all agitated, cold and disheartened. Their legs were burning from the exertion of trudging in the snow and their lungs heaved, with the cold air taking its toll. They had never come across snow before so they did not realise that a normal distance travelled in half a day, would take them a day or so to travel in these conditions. The wind was howling ferociously and the snow pelted them, as if trying to break their spirits. The extreme weather was almost lifelike, as if it was deliberately trying to stop them from getting to their destination. Through the storm they spotted a massive cave up ahead, possibly now only a few hours trek. Its white mass was menacing as it was almost as large as one of their space stations. On seeing the cave, the Commander signalled one of his men. The man veered off to the right to scout ahead, the snow storm ensuring that they could not see him at all after a few metres.

Teller was tending to Chelsea's wounds with the warm water and rags. A large shell of some kind, filled with water, lay to the side of the fire. He had found the shell in the cave, put the snow in it and started a fire, melting the snow into water. The fire had been easy to make, there was more than enough kindling in this cavern. The kindling remotely resembled hair and allowed the fire to burn ferociously. Teller had pulled Chelsea's tank top up, showing all but the nipple on her breasts as he tended to her wounds, including, black swollen and broken ribs. He turned, wringing the blood out of the rags and onto the blackened soil.

Chelsea startled awake at Teller's touch, her voice was croaky and her eyelids so swollen they barely opened. "You could've done it when I was awake. I wouldn't have complained."

"Don't forget you said that! When you get better I will hold you to it." Teller let a small smile come over his face, visible to Chelsea, as his hood no longer covered his feline features.

Chelsea coughed and pain shot through her like fire. "What d'ya do? Beat me when I was sleepin'?"

"No, when you were awake. Don't you remember?"

"How could I forget?"

"Sleeping beauty awakes!" Scrycher walked in from the middle tunnel located behind them, carrying what appeared to be a large spider's leg with thick hairlike follicles covering it. "You forgot that beauty sleep is supposed to make you more beautiful, did you?" He threw the leg into the fire causing it to spark up and the smell of cooking meat to waft through the cavern.

"Ha, ha, Captain. I have something for you." Chelsea gingerly reached into the top of her bosom, scrimmaging around for a while before pulling out a memory stick, silver and shiny.

"Is that what I think it is?"

"Yep."

From the ledge in the caverns wall, Blink's eyes widened. Something so shiny. He had to have it.

"Keep it safe in those then, will you?" Scrycher pointed to her half covered breasts. "Unless you have another use for them, Teller?" Scrycher smiled as Teller blushed, his face bright red as he pulled the tank top back down to cover Chelsea's breast.

The Leopard had been observing the group of men for the better part of their trek across the snow. With too many to attack at once, he waited. He just needed one. He did not have to wait for long...

The military man walked through the snow, obeying his Commander who had given him the signal to scout ahead as he had done a hundred times before. There seemed to be nothing but snow, white snow and more snow. The cave in front of him still looked menacing as though warning them not to venture too near. His senses were all but deadened, the cold had seen to that. He could not see the Leopard sneaking up on him, stalking him and waiting for the right moment. He did not see the Leopard climb the small rock face, or wait above him, until it was too late.

The big cat pounced, its jaw latching around the man's throat, the man's gun went off aimlessly into the air, dropping from his grasp as he was forced to his knees. The Leopard's jaw tightened with the long teeth piercing the man's jugular. No one heard his gurgled screams as the Leopard dragged the body to the ground, using its weight to pin him. The Leopard waited until the hands and feet stopped twitching, until the blood stopped pulsing into his mouth. He then dragged the meal back to his den, to feed his hungry cubs.

"Teller, you were right, the cavern does seem to go on and on, branching off all over the place. It would take days to traverse all the different tunnels."

"The crystal keeps lighting up the middle one, but you say you can't get through?" Teller questioned this. The crystal had been right until now and it had got them to this planet. To come so far and to be stopped by a wall seemed ridiculous to say the least.

"Yeh there is a bloody big wall where the crystal's beam says we need to go. Can't seem to get through, maybe if we had time we…"

There discussion was cut short as the sound of gunfire echoed through the snow.

They were here…

The Commander stopped at the sound of the gunshot, holding up his hand, demanding absolute silence. Everyone stopped in their tracks, with the only sound from them being their chattering teeth, due to the numbing cold. The gunshot echoed through the mountain ranges, then nothing. No scream. No sounds of struggle. Nothing! The Commander knew it was time to act, their surprise attack, no longer a surprise. With silent hand gestures he signalled to two of his men, sending them around the back of the cave. The other two he gestured to the other side of the cave. The remaining man he sent to guard the cave entrance. He made sure each knew the importance of the speed of their assault. The soldiers, happy for this deployment, now ran through the snow, allowing their bodies time to defrost before the attack. Lance and the Gunnery stood still, not speaking, and hoping they would not be deployed. Neither man wanted to be alone or unprotected. They need not have bothered. Their concern was unwarranted as the Commander wanted no issues other than the snow. He definitely did not want two untrained Company men getting in his soldiers' way. With the snow still falling hard, it made the deployment less than acceptable, as once deployed he could not recall his men. All the Commander could do was hope that they were not entering a trap, a trap they could not see.

"You keep the crystal safe, Chelsea." Teller handed it to her, their hands touching briefly as they swapped affectionate glances. The glow from Teller hopped to Chelsea before breaking up into the air around her hand. He then replaced his hood, masking the concern now creeping into his eyes.

"Blinky Boy! Look after her for me, will you?" Scrycher gestured to Chelsea with a nod as he finished getting ready by slinging his beautifully polished rifle over his shoulder.

Blink ear stalks straightened, rotating back and forth to listen for any danger, with his head following their path. His wings rose, to flap slowly in time to his pacing and he bared his little fangs as he growled at the entrance.

"Good boy..."

Chelsea laughed slightly but stopped abruptly, the discomfort obvious on her face as she placed the crystal beside her .

"Chels...?" Scrycher raised an eyebrow, his comment as much as a question as a signal as he reached out to her.

Chelsea composed herself, nodding to show Scrycher that she was OK, as she reached for the pistol he handed her. She pulled back quickly, wincing due to the pain of her broken ribs.

Teller shook his head as Scrycher tried to hand him a pistol. "Don't know how to use one, Captain."

Scrycher avoided Chelsea's stare as he walked over to the ledge to grab the last syringe. He turned, startled by her. She had walked up behind him and spoken, "Boss!" he jumped back slightly and fumbled it.

"Crap." he yelled as he dropped to his knees, only to have Tellers hand appear in between his and the syringe. The two men looked at each other, laughing slightly; knowing how close they came to losing Chelsea's edge.

"That was close." he sighed, accepting the syringe from Teller. He wiped his brow and then injected the drug into Chelsea. "No better time to have you on the top of your game than now." He lowered the syringe, dropping it into the fire and kneeled back down, speaking quietly. "You up for this Teller? You can still back out."

Chelsea's eyes glazed, darting from side to side as the drug took effect. She leant over, intimately rubbing Teller's arm and lifted his hood, looking into his eyes as he looked up. They locked glances... "Uhmmmmm. I am still here," Scrycher cleared his throat as he tried to raise himself from between them, his question still standing as he repeated. "Teller?"

Teller snapped out of his trance; rising up, he remembered the dilemma that lay before them. "As I said before, we have little choice in the matter." He skulked out of the cave entrance and into the snow storm, knowing the Company men would be here soon to kill them all...

Lance's mind raced as he walked through the snow and towards the cave. His thoughts drifted to memories of his mates, the pub he liked so much and the job he had trained for... a lawyer. He wanted this nightmare to be over and he still did not want to be a Captain. *It will be over soon!* he thought.

The Commander trudged beside Lance, his eyes blinked rapidly in the cold winds, combing what little of the environment he could see, through the blizzard. His teeth chattered, not from the nervousness he felt from his unknown surroundings, but from the cold. He forced his mouth closed, listening through the howling winds as he caught a glimpse of something glinting above the cave. His right arm reached out, stopping Lance from taking a step further as he peered into the direction of the movement. Patiently, he waited, signalling Lance to be quiet as he opened his mouth to speak. He needed to make sure this went down without a hitch and that they got back to the ship in one piece with a Captain, a live Captain; and hopefully one that knew when to shut up. He glared back as Lance opened his mouth to speak again, ensuring Lance knew that he was not impressed. He knew better than to blame his imagination for the movement ahead, however he was pretty sure they were not at risk; for now. "Shut up, and stay behind me. If you can do that, you may just stay alive long enough for me to get you back to that father of yours. It would not be a good career choice for me if I had to explain, how I let his son die on this unforgiving wasteland."

The Gunnery smirked as he walked off to the left of them. He was trying to think of a way to get every one of the criminals killed, *maybe put them between the Captain and the Commander?* Of course, he would have to distance himself from them to make sure he was safe. While fumbling with his pistol, several other scenarios flowed through his head, but none as amusing. If only the Captain had ordered them killed, this would all be over a lot quicker.

Two of the soldiers walked around the side of the cave. They were cautious now and looking out for a trap. Their numb fingers rested, at the ready, on the triggers of their rifles. They could not see much in this blizzard so their goal was to get a vantage point and cover the suspected battlefield. They climbed high and were almost out of breath by the time they turned to look at each other. Nodding, they agreed on a flat, high point above the cave from where they could sniper almost anyone moving to or from the cave. One of the men dropped to his knees. The snow covered his body and seeped through his uniform as he lay down in it. Now wet and cold he looked over the area through his scope as he shivered. The other man continued standing in order to keep guard above him.

Teller lay perfectly still, as he did not want to give away his position. He had buried himself in the snow so he could not be seen, could not be captured. His cloak and fur protected him from the extreme cold as he waited with his eyes closed. His mind swelled with thoughts of ways out of this situation. He did not want to kill these men, there had to be another way. He would only kill if it was life and death and at this moment, it was not.

"Hey, I can see Gordo. He's almost at the cave entrance." The soldier lying on the snow had not taken his eyes off the scope as he followed the soldier below. The man was moving to position himself at the cave entrance.

The standing soldier lowered his rifle for a moment as he spoke jovially, "I heard they've got a woman. You think he'll get a chance to have his way with her before we get us some?"

These were poorly chosen words and the last words he ever spoke. Teller burst out of the snow in a fit of rage, ripping the man's throat out before he finished the sentence. Blood sprayed over the other soldier as he lay on the floor and still observed the actions below through his scope. One of the two claws left on Teller's right hand was stuck in his victim's windpipe, ripping it from his finger as the man fell to the bloodied snow. The remaining soldier rolled onto his back with his weapon raised at Teller. Teller's other hand slashed at the man, his claws, shredding the rifle's shaft as if it were paper.

"Surrender and I will spare your life." Teller's pleaded as he spoke.

The soldier reached for his pistol in the front of his vest, drew it and pointed it towards Teller. A shot rang out. Teller sidestepped easily and much faster than the eye could see, avoiding the bullet with ease. The soldier did not get off another shot. He fumbled, trying to re-cocked the gun, then gurgled. The single claw remaining on Teller's right hand had been rammed through his windpipe and out the other side, hitting his spine and cutting through the bone. Teller raised himself from his kneeling position, removing this claw from the dead man's throat. He shook, the shock of the scene before him sinking in as he stared at his hand and then at the red stained snow around him. *What have I done?* He could not ponder this for long as he had to get to Chelsea, her welfare was more important than anything else, even his conscience.

The pain from the missing claw did not matter as he bounded down the side of the cave. All he could see was Chelsea being manhandled by the guard, this clouded his judgement as his temper flared and he gained speed. Sliding he came down the side of the mountain, just outside the cave. He did not see the rifle until it was too late.

The Commander stood above him as his mind fogged. "I knew I saw something."

Chelsea heard the entry of the man and raised her gun with both hands, trying to steady it. She was still weak but knew how to handle a weapon and the drugs were making her forget about the pain for now; but they also made her very jumpy, almost paranoid. She waited. Nothing! They came no closer. A body stumbled into the cave. Chelsea shot at the man who wearily tried to dodge the bullet. It scraped his arm and he yelped.

"Chelsea."

She lowered the gun, shocked at the figure before her. Teller was groggily standing there, unable to do anything but call her name.

"If you want him to stay alive, drop your gun and come out now." The Commander walked in with his rifle cocked and aimed at Teller's head. *One false move and we are both dead.* Chelsea thought. A soldier circled behind Chelsea, taking the gun from her drooped hands as her head dropped in defeat. The man pushed her violently towards the entrance of the cave and the small memory stick glinted in the fire as it fell from her breasts.

"You..." She swore under her breath as he pushed her again.

Blink watched quietly from his vantage point. His scales were hackled but he dared not make a sound. *Too many,* he thought as he watched the shiny, silver stick, fall to the floor. His ears pricked up as if he heard something. He waited, his ears twitching, and then he blinked away.

The two other soldiers cut across the front of the cave, close enough to see the entrance but not to be seen. "This will be an easy kill," the leading guard snickered as he quickened his pace. Flanking these criminals was all he cared about.

"But we have been given orders to take them prisoner."

"Since when has anyone taken orders on this command?"

The trailing soldier shrugged his shoulders, "Well, you've got a point."

The two men made it around the side of the cave but there was no vantage there. They could not take a defensive stance as the walls were too high and there were no ledges to get up onto. They turned to head back. The snow had eased a little, but was still enough to conceal Scrycher who caused them to step back in surprise as he jumped out of the crack in the cave wall, pulling his rifle on them.

Scrycher knew this was not going to be easy as both men were armed and he had no cover to protect him. He thanked the planet for his advantages, the snow, surprise and the darkness of the planet itself. He jumped from the alcove, rotating his rifle and activating the blade. The soldier reacted, stepping backwards and receiving the blade square in his chest. The blow knocked him further back with Scrycher's rifle and blade combination lodged in his chest. Scrycher slipped on a rock that had been concealed by the snow. He failed to hold onto the rifle. It slipped from his grasp as he tried pulling the blade out, but it quickly fell out of his reach as the body fell to the ground. The remaining soldier needed no second chance. He acted decisively, reaching into his jacket to pull out a large knife and brandished it at Scrycher. Scrycher reacted faster, and deflected the blow with his forearm. A small amount of blood spilled through Scrycher's jacket. Scrycher kicked the legs from under the man, he fell onto him and they rolled on the snowy ground, both struggling for the knife. They regained their footing as they pushed at each other, finally raising themselves to their feet. The soldier had gained better footing and kicked Scrycher in the shins. Scrycher stumbled forward. This was all the advantage the guard needed to slash again at Scrycher. This time the blade made contact, hitting his chest, drawing blood and splitting open the pocket Blink had been using for his treasures. The trinkets spilled to the snow in a light tinkle, barely audible in the howling winds.

Blink heard this tinkle and appeared on the snow next to his shinies. He was just in time to see the guard lung forward to overbalance Scrycher with his momentum.

"Die, you half breed," he yelled as he thrust the knife down for the final blow.

Blink disappeared again and in that instant the soldier clutched at his face. The dagger flailed aimlessly, cutting Scrycher's cheek as he rolled to get out of the way. Scrycher righted himself to watch with his balance regained. The soldier pulled at his face and head, screaming until he finally dropped the knife. Blink's claws ripped at the man's eyes, then ripped into his skull and pulled out clumps of hair, while screeching like a wild bird. The sharp little tail flailed around erratically as the man screamed a blood curdling cry and his nose dropped from his face, splayed off with Blink's tail. The man reached higher, trying to get Blink off. The harder he tried, the deeper Blink's claws dug in. Scrycher picked up the knife. With a feeling of pity coming over him, he slashed the soldier's throat in an act of mercy; but he ensured that he did not go near Blink's panicked body as his tail still flailed erratically. The blood from the cuts on the soldier spilled over the snow, staining it red and framing the carnage. As the body dropped to the ground Blink continued his frenzy.

Scrycher walked over to the first soldier's corpse, which was now partially covered in snow. He put his boot on the man's chest and wrenched his weapon out, pausing only to wipe the blade on his arm as he allowed it to retract. He then composed himself, airing calmness as he walked over to

Blink. He hoped this would help calm Blink as he still frenzied over the soldier's dead corpse. No flesh remained on the man's face, only bone. Deeply gouged bone.

"It's over Blink. It's over." Scrycher's voice was soft as though he was talking to a baby. Blink, who was covered in blood, innocently looked up with his big white eyes and then he blinked away.

Scrycher looked around for something to patch his pocket. He was sure that the two Company pins from the soldiers' uniforms were not going to be missed. Then he replaced Blinks trinkets -every last one - before he started to head to the front of the cave. He stopped walking for a second as he felt a shift in the weight of his pocket. He opened it slowly, the huge white eyes looked up at him, pleading for forgiveness. Gently he stoked the little dragons head, reassuring him everything would be alright. But he had no idea of the ambush awaiting them.

Chapter 8

"He is innocent!" Scrycher's voice was rough and strained as he gestured towards Teller. "He has done nothing wrong. I took him prisoner, forced him to work for me... You must let him go... I will surrender." His voice lowered at the end of the sentence indicating to those who listened that he had given up hope, when in reality he did not want to surrender. He had a plan even though he had been caught unawares! He had come running down from the side of the cave to find Teller and Chelsea apprehended. The soldier guarding Chelsea had been surprised by this, giving Chelsea enough time to turn the rifle on the man, which she crashed across his face.

"As will I." Chelsea lowered the soldier's gun to the ground and raised her hands above her head again.

The soldier who was now behind her raised himself from the ground into a kneeling position. He spat and watched as two of his teeth sprayed onto the snow with the blood. As the teeth disappeared into the snow, he raised himself completely and walked in front of her. Leaning forward he picked up the rifle and addressed Chelsea. "Cow!" he said, in an all too aggressive tone, as he walked to position himself behind her again, and swing the rifle into the side of her head. Chelsea collapsed forward as blood oozed from a partially healed wound on the side of her cheek. The crystal became air born as the collision and subsequent fall forced it from her cleavage. Its glow lit the battle area as it sailed through the air to land at Scrycher's feet.

As she raised herself, Chelsea saw the glint in Scrycher's eye and knew he had a plan. Because of this, she did not retaliate. She waited, hoping that this guard would feel her wrath again before this was over.

In an all too slow and non-threatening way, Scrycher moved forward and bent down to pick up the crystal. He did not want to get shot, but he needed to get this crystal to Teller. If he managed to get Teller released, he knew that it would only be a matter of time before he would find that one thing they had missed in order to complete their goal. Scrycher was going to make damn sure that he had given Teller the crystal to help him complete the all too important task. As he grasped the crystal in his right hand, a tingling sensation coursed through his open wound. The crystal's light lowered considerably. It sensed the danger at hand, feeding Scrycher its power in anticipation of the battle.

"This man is but a Story Teller for his people, he uses this mere crystal to tell of their past. You would not deny them of that... would you?" Scrycher gestured towards Teller with the crystal, all the time sounding very convincing in his plea.

Lance knew that this Teller, a Stray, was not a part of his original orders. He also knew that too much of the past had been lost from cultures assimilated into the Company and he was not about to let more of it be lost on this godforsaken frozen tomb.

Scrycher moved towards Teller, with his arm outstretched, in an attempt to hand the crystal to him. He was unaware that its glow had diminished greatly, as it had deposited most of its energy into him. "I hand you back your lineage. Use it wisely to find what you are looking for." Scrycher knew this was their best course of action. If it came down to it and the Company men had him and Chelsea in custody, then they would hopefully not bother with Teller; giving him the chance to finish their quest.

Teller stretched out his hand.

"That's far enough now, or I'll blow your hand off!" The Commander was getting nervous. This young Captain Dragoon was compromising this capture by doing nothing but listening to this man.

Scrycher gently lobbed the crystal to Teller and stepped backwards to his original position. *Click, Click, Click,* nervously the safeties of the guns trained on Scrycher and his crew were removed and stances changed so the men were ready to fire if anyone did anything suspicious.

Cupping his hands, Teller caught the crystal and protected it from any unwanted observations.

"We can all calm down now, can't we?" Lance's voice crackled nervously, and his hands shook. He tried to hide it, but with this many guns with safeties off, he did not feel safe! It was all he could do to stop himself from throwing up. "I accept your terms of surrender. The Story Teller can go, but only once you are cuffed and in my custody."

The Commander looked at Lance with raised eyebrows. This was an easy capture and they had almost apprehended them all. Why negotiate at all? Especially when this man had nothing over them and nothing to negotiate with!

Lance reiterated. "Is this alight with you, Commander? Then we can all go home, safe and sound." Lance's eyes spoke too, the Commander knew he could not convince him to do otherwise.

"Yes, Captain Dragoon! I am alright with this surrender. I am sure your father will be pleased to see you return with these two."

Lance was quick and cutting in reply. "I do not care what my father thinks!"

Scrycher saw this as the opening he required and took it, pushing his way back into the conversation. "Well, we do have something else you may want, other than our capture that is."

"What?" The Commander had seen this type of negotiation before. It never ended well.

Scrycher made eye contact with Lance. "Captain Dragoon! I feel there is no love lost on your father, so I put this to you. On our ship, on a memory stick, we have information leading us to believe your father is performing a great deal of illegal activities."

"Sorry, what are you saying?"

"You spent three months chasing us across the galaxy, and your father is the real one you should have been chasing."

"How do you know this?"

"We have been collecting information on him for years."

"Like what?"

"Like the slave trade of Strays, the hunting of them, and the senseless butchering of Stray children. We have records of all this, and it points directly to *Lord Dragoon!*" Scrycher could see he was getting through to Lance. He could see the doubts going through his mind, on his face and in his eyes.

"And where is this information now?"

"Can we make a deal? Let us go in exchange for the information?" Scrycher had played all he was going to for now until he got a definite answer.

Lance turned to the Commander, whispering. "Do you think they are bluffing?" The Commander had been on the Company vessel long enough to know this was more fact than fiction.

He shook his head. This would have been a bold action even for a criminal. To boast this without some hard evidence would be a death sentence in itself. "No, I reckon they might just have it."

"Show me this information."

Scrycher looked over to Chelsea, giving her a nod. She reached deep into her bosom and all the men ogled at her ample cleavage. She fiddled for what seemed like an eternity but did not find the memory stick. She turned to Scrycher. "Sorry Boss, the memory stick must have fallen out with the crystal." She turned her head towards the soldier behind her, a cranky look in her eye. "Maybe if this prat was not so heavy handed then we'd have it now."

Lance shrugged, looking at the ground where the crystal had been, it would take hours to comb through the snow in order to find the memory device. "Take them into custody, all of them, until we can find it."

"Hold your own there young man… Blink!"

Blink poked his huge eyes and tiny head out of the pocket he had been hiding in. He knew that tone... he was in trouble. His little clawed paws fumbled with the shiny memory stick he had removed from the cavern earlier. The one that had fallen from Chelsea's breasts in the scuffle, and now he brought it to the top of Scrycher's pocket.

"Thank you very much, little boy." Scrycher raised his hand to take the memory stick from Blink. Blink looked around nervously and with all the guns pointing at him, he fumbled; accidentally dropping the stick into the snow beside Scrycher's gun. Scrycher responded quickly as he innocently bent down, trying to get the memory stick before it melted its way any further into the snow.

This was the chance the Gunnery needed. He had positioned his pistol so it was trained on Scrycher for the whole capture and now it was time to use it. He recalled the conversation with the cloaked figure on the ship… *"We cannot take any chances. All of the criminals must be dead before you leave that planet, or you will not receive payment!"*

He pulled the trigger as if in response to Scrycher's movement.

Blink, in his nervousness after dropping the shiny stick, scoured the armed men with his beady eyes. One of these men caught his attention, the Gunnery. This man had his gun trained on Scrycher, and sweat beaded down his face in this cold place. No one else seemed to notice. Blink did not take his eyes off him, did not even blink. The Gunnery pulled on the trigger. Blink was fast to react. He blinked from the pocket to the Gunnery's weapon, knocking the aim off and then immediately blinked back into Scrycher's pocket.

With its original target compromised, the bullet crashed into Scrycher's shoulder blade, shattering the bone on impact. Combat worn, Scrycher spun his body, trying to cushion the impact of the bullet. As he was spinning, he dropped his body, lowering his centre of gravity; allowing him to remove the dagger in his boot with his right hand. His motion carried him a full circle up out of the spin to flick the dagger at the Gunnery. As he let go of the dagger he felt the power from his blood flow into it, engulfing it. A bright energy ball released from where the dagger had been.

The throw was precise and the dagger, the energy ball, hit the Gunnery's chest precisely where Scrycher had aimed. The smell of burning flesh was intense. All present gagged at the stench. Gunnery still stood upright with wide eyes. *What just happened?* He dropped the small pistol he had shot seconds earlier and clutched at his chest. Unable to find anything to clutch, he dropped to his knees; for where his chest had been was now a hole. The flesh was burnt, cauterised instantly, and no blood flowed. With his eyes still open, he fell forward into the snow to sleep forever... Dreaming of beer wenches and riches.

The Commander stood looking in shock as the snow filled the hole in the Gunneries chest briefly and then melted. He had not seen anything like this before. *Who is this freak? How can he do this thing?* Those were the last things he thought before all hell broke loose.

Chelsea saw her chance and dropped to the floor, grabbing at the blade she had in her shoe. As she stood up with the knife ready to defend herself, her eyes glazed. She was too slow, a combination of wounds and drugs, dulling her normally impressive reflexes. She dropped the knife, her hands covered in blood and two bullet holes in her chest.

The Commander did not waste a second, shooting Chelsea twice in the chest before she could use her blade. He did not see Teller arching his back. The soldier who was standing behind Chelsea did, though, and was quick to react, shooting Teller in the chest with his rifle. His aim was perfect but did not hit Teller in the heart as he had arched so quickly.

Teller looked in disbelief as Chelsea's lifeless body hit the snow. He saw the Commander move his aim to Scrycher. Still holding the crystal Teller arched violently, hissing as he did. He did not feel the bullet hit the crystal, shattering part of it in his hand. Both the crystal particles and bullet pierced his chest. He did not feel the bullet puncture an artery from his heart and lodge itself in the bone behind it with fragments of the crystal scattered along its path. All he could feel was the acid spit, a natural defensive response, flowing from his stomach and through his open mouth as he hurled it at the Commander. His body arched completely forward, projecting the spit so fast no one had time to move.

The Commander clutched his face in agony. He dropped the useless rifle that the acid had eaten through in seconds. The rest of the acid had sprayed onto his hands and face; burning through them. The smell of his burning flesh, mixing with the Gunnery's, was overwhelming. The acid corroded the Commander's face, eating through his skull to his brain as he held his head, his fingers corroding to the bone and falling apart as he screamed for mercy. No mercy came as he pleaded for quick relief in the cold darkness of death.

Scrycher's pain was unnoticeable as he saw Teller crash to the floor with the crystal hugged close to his wound and covered in his blood. Blood that was pulsing out of him in a stream, to pool in the snow beneath him. Scrycher reacted by grabbing his rifle from the ground. Still kneeling he had the perfect vantage as he fired at the soldier that had been behind Chelsea, the one that had just shot Teller. The guard did not get off another shot. Scrycher's rifle fired, once, twice, three times. The guard fell backwards with blood gurgling from his mouth, his punctured lungs filled with blood. He did not see who shot him nor did he care as his lifeless body hit the snow...

Scrycher turned towards the Commander, and Lance. The Commander was gripping his face and a sound was coming through his fingers. An agonising scream filled the air as the flesh melted from them, the bones dropping in the snow beside his feet. He saw Lance grab his weapon and reacted. He drew his rifle, activating the blade and slicing at Lance's calf, unable to do much else from the kneeling position he was in. He only wanted to wound Lance as he needed Lance to return with his information. To give it to the Councill. Shooting him was not an option. He could feel the cold blade cut deep, and could see the blood, followed by the shock in Lance's eyes, and his trembling hands.

Lance head flew forward to cover the snow in vomit. He did not know if it was the unbearable stench of burning flesh or the acid burns to the left of his face, accidental splashes from the attack on the Commander. Confused and petrified he raised himself shakily and drew his pistol. Adrenalin made him react rather than act. He saw the blade from Scrycher's rifle extending from the butt and felt it bite into his flesh. Felt himself pull the trigger, again and again. The bullets went smashing into Scrycher's chest, ripping the life from him. This was the last thing Lance saw before his body dropped to the snow in shock.

Scrycher smiled as the first bullet crashed into his chest. What a bizarre world this was! They were so close to their goal, so close… He thought of the friends made, and of the friends lost. Of that pesky little dragon, and what would have happened if he had not taken, then dropped the memory stick. Of everyone and everything, he had touched. He felt another *thump*. His chest beat again then another *thump*. He looked up at Lance who was still shaking violently out of fear and pain, the adrenalin fuelling him on. *How funny is this?* he thought. With a smile on his face he looked at Lance. Lance was his hope to bring down Lord Dragoon. Maybe there would be something good out of this. He fell backwards into the snow. Backwards as with this last action, he ensured that he did not crush what was still hiding in his pocket, that pesky little dragon. *Blink!*

Chapter 9

The storm had subsided and the sky was now clear. Without the snowfall, the fire from the cave illuminated the surrounding snow and the bodies strewn across it. It had ended! Just like that. In one last desperate battle. Teller lay mortally wounded, the snow a cold comfort, numbing the pain. His heart was still pumping his life force, his blood, from the small hole in his chest; the blood pulsing over the crystal and into the snow. He held the cracked crystal in his hand, close to his body, looking intimate in his embrace… It had been broken by the force of the gunshot and shards of it were embedded in his flesh and even in passing, a faint glow still illuminated the crystal's core as it rested its last rest in Teller's hand. They comforted each other as his eyes began to discolour and he slowly lost consciousness. His blood soaked deeper in the snow to become frozen in an intricate latticework of crystals. His eyes had remained open to stare blankly at the crystal. The crystal responded, dulling further. Then the light in the crystal blinked out. In that instant so did his, their life force disappearing from the shells that held them.

Blink awoke in the cold, his little body shivering. He could not feel the warmth of Scrycher's body any more, as it had been hours since the fight. No noise could be heard, no *thump, thump, thump*, of Scrycher's chest. Blink clawed frantically at the pocket, dislodging a Company clip and spilling his trinkets on the snow. He forced his head out after the trinkets, observing all that was still. He shivered further at the sight of bodies, yet there was no smell reminding him of their horrific demise.

Cautiously, he clawed his way out of the dark pocket; the remaining clip holding it loosely together was easily broken. He emerged, his colour jet black. As he scurried across the snow, his colour changed to white, his eyes still white and beady, curiously searching for something. He saw the man. The bad man. The one that had tried to capture them. Hurriedly he ran over to him, stopping near his face and sniffing. There was no sign of breath and no sign of life. Blink cocked his leg to urinate on his face and pee dripped off and into the snow, melting it. Lance's eyes blinked open! Blink jumped, scared out of his little mind and screeching as he quickly ran away. Blink's eyes did not leave Lance until he collided with Teller's body.

Teller's lifeless body lay in the cold snow. The broken crystal had now fallen from his hand and rested in the crystallised pool of blood. The reflection from the crystal attracted Blinks attention, and he forgot about Lance. Wearily, he crept closer to the crystal with his head moving from side to side, stalking his prey. He paused until he could see there was no other movement, then focused on the crystal. This was pretty, very pretty. It would go nicely with the rest of his treasure. *Not as pretty as before, broken.* But Blink didn't mind, it was pretty none the less. Blink crawled cautiously to the crystal, but forgot caution as his tongue darted out to encircle it. His tongue was slightly cut by the damaged crystal and his blood dropped into the crystals core. More blood dripped from his tongue until the blood overflowed to fall upon the crystalline form of Teller's blood. Blink screeched at the pain and he tried to let go, shaking his head vigorously from side to side. This sped up the loss of blood and his colour returned to black, then blue. His white eyes blackened as a film formed over them and then his body greyed as the remainder of his life was consumed by the crystal. Then he was gone, in a BLINK...

The blood glowed; thawing itself so it could flow again. Down, down, down, deep within the snow. It travelled deep within the reaches of the earth, trying to find a place to rest. Finally, it stopped, resting on a dome. A crystalline dome. The blood pooled there waiting. Waiting for a chance to enter.

The pain in his leg was excruciating as Lance tried to open his eyes. His consciousness had been revived by a warm feeling on his face and he extended his tongue. The taste was salty; he wondered what it could be as he finally got his eyes to open. The little dragon, that obviously did not realise he was still alive, jumped and bolted away from him. *That little dragon just pissed on me, well I will...*

His thoughts were cut short. The little dragon had its attention was drawn elsewhere. It had crashed into the Story Teller's body, then walked over to the crystal; hooked it with its tongue and then struggled slightly. It now lay dead. "That's karma you little rodent," he mumbled as he raised himself, only to fall down again. The wound to his leg was deep. He had not bled out, thankfully, as the blood had stopped flowing in the cold, but the pain was still there. He raised himself onto a knee and then dragged himself between the bodies. Lance found what he needed to make a crutch using a couple of the rifles and bandaged his leg with a shirt off one of the men. He trudged off slowly, trying to keep the weight off his leg. The pain shot out again as he forgot to favour it. He knew the journey would be long but his only thoughts went to his own survival.

The black, hooded figure appeared in the ship. He was to wait in the room he had met the Gunnery many times during this chase. Patiently, he felt the table beneath him. This hooded man had made several trips here in the last few days and he was sure no one had survived, not even his son. The death of his son was exactly what he wanted! Lord Dragoon laid his palms on the table. Both of them were bare of skin as though it had been flayed from them. *Click*, a compartment opened in the middle of the table. As it opened a light emanated from within. A light similar to that of Teller's crystal, but somehow corrupt. Visions of the planet below formed within the crystals' light. Crystals dotted the landscape, many of them burnt by the ships impact; but they were there. Lord Dragoon's head lurched backwards laughing an eerie, dreadful laugh. As his head flicked back, his hood fell off. The features! How could it be? It was Lance's face with longer hair. "Finally I have found you, after a hundred years of searching, you were here all the time. The Crystal Planet… my destiny! I will be back to claim you. Once I convince the Councill to let Lance take my place, as the head of the Company. A reward for finding this place. I will assume his identity. I will bring him, no… me, back to claim you as my own." His voice had become evil and menacing, his mind corrupt after five hundred years of life. Five hundred years of deceiving the Councill, of killing off his youngest son from each pairing then surrendering his role to them. A dead son. Always assuming their identity immediately in the role at the head of the Councill again. His plan never failed, no one ever questioned. His thoughts of true evil flowed from him as he laid his palms on the crystal and he gave it directions, telling it what to do next.

Lance struggled on. It had been days since the fight and the deep cut in his leg ached badly as the infection set in. Sweat dripped from his body, even in this cold place, as his own blood carried the poison. With all this pain, he had still struggled to get back to the shuttle, at times crawling, others hopping and finally dragging himself, trying where possible to use the crude crutch. As he travelled his thoughts were clouded at best, but his thoughts were still there. *I will never ever be a man of compassion again. Or a military man. Back to the life of luxury for me.* His ideals were not living up to the reality of the past three months. He dropped down onto his hands in front of the shuttle. "Finally!" he screamed.

Wirrrrrrrrrr, clunk, the shuttle's open door raised itself and closed. Lance's heart jumped! He let go of the crutch and lunged at the hatch door. His fists banged at it in an attempt to get the attention of someone inside as the shuttle powered up. *Who is inside?* He did not know. A forceful and mistimed blow caused a finger to break and pierce his bleeding hands. The engines from the shuttle warmed the ground around him, warming him, then searing everything as it slowly lifted off. Lance could feel his flesh being burnt. He could smell himself being cooked. Cooked alive as his hair was now gone and his flesh blistered off his body. His only thought left, *WHY ME?* as he fell to the ground to be scorched further by the shuttle. His body was now just a shell, now not even resembling Lance. The shell, a blistering corpse beyond recognition.

The shuttle returned to the docking bay after its long journey. Its entry echoing in the crew-less Company vessel. The two vessels readied themselves for the long and lonely journey ahead of them as the main ship turned and headed for home. It was answering its master's call, returning home; with its current coordinates stored for its return.

The blood's glow had intensified and its frequency of pulsing had changed over the days of waiting on the crystal dome. It… they were now glowing and pulsating in unison with the dome, which glowed and pulsated in turn as if one with the blood. As they pulsed together, the blood oozed through the dome. It dropped down, deeper, deeper, into the dark unknown. Finally, it lay there resting, resting in the darkness. In that darkness the blood glowed brilliantly illuminating the space it occupied. The outline of the object was that of a branch, a large branch of a huge tree. What it was doing this far down we do not know. But this is where the blood had been drawn and it lay there, content and satisfied. It had reached its destination. The peace was short lived. The tree lit up in brilliant light, the chamber beneath it obvious. This chamber, like a coffin, housed a sleeping Stray. The tree absorbed the blood and all its life force and the life force awakened the tree from its deep slumber. Absorbing the blood into itself it came to life dramatically as images flashed forth, filling the room, illuminating the many chambers on its walls. Images of pain, death, wrong choices, of ships in battle, fighting, snow, blizzards, ships falling, falling, then finally red, blood red as the life drained from the body, the mind waning away. Then came two others. Their life force overpowering. Their need for conclusion strong. The red flashed more intently; blinding, like the sun itself, intense beyond belief, burning, and burning all in its way. Then nothing. As quick as the light appeared it was diminished, *blinking* out the last hope, last life, to be gone forever. Leaving the tree as it had found it…

In darkness!

The End Or A New Beginning?

Line art by Karis Tobias
DA: minti-fresh.deviantart.com/
tumblr: coolmintifresh.tumblr.com/

Teller fan art by Shelley McCaw

Teller fan art by Shelley McCaw

Blink fan art by Shelley McCaw

Artwork by Stephen Landry

Artwork by Stephen Landry
www.Facebook.com/StephenLandryArt

Other works by DC Daines

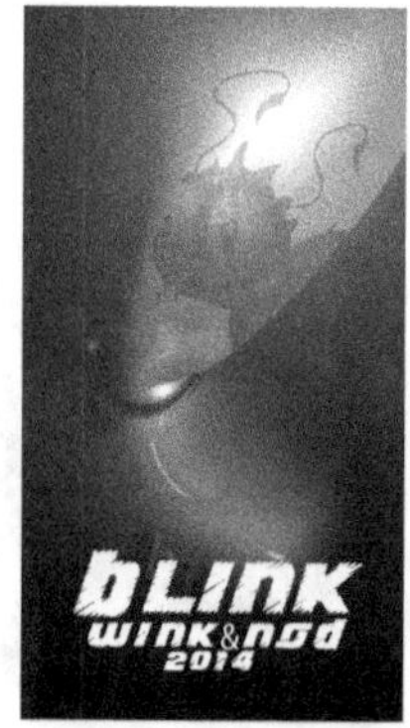